What
Counts
as Love

The

John

Simmons

Short

Fiction

Award

University of

Iowa Press

Iowa City

*Marian
Crotty*

*What
Counts
as Love*

University of Iowa Press, Iowa City 52242

www.uipress.uiowa.edu
Printed in the United States of America

The University of Iowa Press is a member of Green Press
Initiative and is committed to preserving natural resources.

Printed on acid-free paper

Library of Congress Cataloging-in-Publication Data
Names: Crotty, Marian, 1980– author.
Title: What counts as love / Marian Crotty.
Description: Iowa City : University Of Iowa Press, [2017] |
Series: John Simmons Short Fiction Award | Series: Iowa
Short Fiction Award
Identifiers: LCCN 2017005562 | ISBN 978-1-60938-516-3 (pbk) |
ISBN 978-1-60938-517-0 (ebk)
Subjects: | BISAC: FICTION / Short Stories (single author).
Classification: LCC PS3603.R6797 A6 2017 | DDC 813/.6—dc23
LC record available at https://lccn.loc.gov/2017005562

Contents

ACKNOWLEDGMENTS

Earlier versions of some stories appeared in the following publications: "Crazy for You" in *Confrontation*, "The Fourth Fattest Girl at Cutting Horse Ranch" in *Third Coast*, "The Common Application with Supplement" in *Alaska Quarterly Review*, "A Real Marriage" in *Southern Review*, "The Next Thing that Happens" in *Washington Square*, "A New Life" and "What Counts as Love" in *The Potomac Review*, and "Kindness" in *Kenyon Review*.

Many people and organizations have helped me with this book, providing not just feedback and funding, but also encouragement, friendship, and inspiration. I am especially grateful to the following: My teachers and mentors, including Pam Durban, T. M. McNally, Jewell Parker Rhodes, Melissa Pritchard, Ron Carlson, Julianna Baggott, Elizabeth Stuckey-French, Bob Shacochis, and, in particular, Mark Winegardner.

To my writer friends Sophie Rosenblum, Jake Wolff, Katie Cortese, and Want Chyi who read earlier versions of these stories and offered invaluable feedback. To my friends from Arizona State, especially Caitlin Horrocks, Todd Kaneko, Elizabyth Hiscox, and Doug Jones, and everyone from Florida State, especially John Wang, Kilby Allen, Brenda Peynado, and Micah Dean Hicks.

To the editors of the literary journals who edited and published my stories.

Thank you to my colleagues and students in the writing department at Loyola University Maryland.

I am very grateful for financial support from Florida State University, Arizona State University, Loyola University Maryland, Theresa A. Wilhoit, the Bread Loaf Writers' Conference, the Sewanee Writers' Conference, the Camargo Foundation, and the Corporation of Yaddo.

Thank you to my good friends Crystal Massey and Lynn Paul who always make me laugh and think. Thank you to my parents and my sisters for your support and encouragement. And, most of all, thank you to Melissa for being in my life.

What
Counts
as Love

Crazy
for
You

That summer, while Emily's mom painted pictures of Iranian militiamen in the garage, we watched Sarah Morrison have sex. Sarah rented the casita behind the Freedman's pool shed, a tiny stucco building with just enough room for a bed and desk—a little alcove in the corner with a hot plate and a minifridge. She took classes at Arizona State and wore pink tights under frayed jeans cut off at the swell of her thighs. Emily thought she looked like Madonna with long curly hair and slightly less eye makeup, but I said she was prettier. From the window in the Freedman's bathroom, with Emily's Nikon bird-watching binoculars, we could see everything.

In the mornings and evenings, he was a milky white redhead

with a sunken space in his chest. The guy in the afternoons looked about as unassuming as the first guy, but when he took off his clothes, it was all sweat and testosterone: a broad back and twitching muscles, a look on his face like he might eat Sarah alive without saying a word.

Emily said she liked the redhead better because he was Sarah's boyfriend and because he'd helped her make a mousetrap-powered car for the fifth-grade science fair the year before, but this was because Emily was boring. When I told her I liked Kirk Cameron, she said her celebrity crush was a tie between Jonas Salk and Simon Wiesenthal.

"The Nazi Hunter?" she said. "Don't you know about the Nuremburg Trials?"

The redhead always came over with a stack of textbooks and spent hours behind Sarah's typewriter. When they did have sex, it looked like the diagrams of procreation I'd seen in the slideshow at Woman Readiness Day the spring before—the two of them staring off in their own directions as if they were each imagining the mystery of the egg leaving the fallopian tube. Mr. Afternoon made Sarah wriggle like a half-dead fish.

After, we'd lie on the floorboards in Emily's room picturing their blurry pink-white bodies and imagining what they said to each other. Emily said Sarah was in love with the redhead and was only hanging around with Mr. Afternoon to be nice, that Mr. Afternoon came from a bad family and Sarah felt sorry for him.

"Oh, Sarah," Emily would say, dropping her chin to make her voice sound deep. "I can't believe a girl as smart as you lets me kiss her. Your family would hate it."

I said Mr. Afternoon was a Russian mobster who liked Sarah because she reminded him of his wife who'd died of scurvy.

"They don't have scurvy," she said. "It's a modern country, too, you know."

"She was very poor," I said. "She only ate stale bread and garbage."

"Maybe," she said. "I guess if she was an orphan."

It had been Mrs. Freedman's idea for Emily and me to hang out. My mom had been cleaning the Freedman's house two times a week for years, but Mrs. Freedman hadn't met me until that spring when I got tonsillitis and my mom made me come to all of the houses with her. Most of the places were empty with a key under the mat and a note on the kitchen counter with instructions, but Mrs. Freedman spent two hours grilling me about school and telling me I had good bone structure. After that, she kept inviting me over.

"The woman's a moron," my mom said. "She thinks you're going to help her fat kid become skinny. This is the problem with women like that. They marry for money and then get pissed off when they have ugly kids."

But my mom made me hang out with Emily anyway. Her boyfriend, Rick, had been sleeping over more often, and when he woke up, he liked the apartment to be quiet.

Plus, my mom said spending time with a private school kid and her rich, educated parents would improve my chances of getting a college scholarship. "If they give you a book, you take it," she said. "If they say a word you don't know, you write it down and look it up when you get home."

I pretended to hate the Freedmans as much as my mom did, but the truth was I liked being in a house where the soap came wrapped in flowered paper and where people disagreed without yelling at each other. Hanging out with Emily was better than being alone in the apartment with Rick, who was always farting out loud and making me wash soggy cornflakes out of his cereal bowls.

Mrs. Freedman left us alone unless she heard us rummaging in the freezer, looking for Mr. Freedman's Klondike bars, and then her ears perked up. At eleven years old, Emily was already wearing a size fourteen in women's clothing, and Mrs. Freedman was afraid that any misstep would push her not-yet-teenager into plus sizes.

"Emily," she would call out. "Come here. Let me see you," and I would follow Emily into the garage where Mrs. Freedman would be drinking a glass of wine and squinting at an oil painting of an Iranian soldier shrouded in a homemade paper mask, throwing his hands up toward the burning city behind him. "Don't you want to play outside?" she would say. "Don't you want to swim?"

Sometimes I would ask questions about the paintings hanging from wire cables. The creepiest one showed a woman in a long black dress and headscarf standing behind a pile of blown-up dead people, holding a rifle and staring at me with wide blank eyes like she was expecting to die any minute and didn't care. I wanted to know why these people were killing each other and if anything like this had ever happened in America, but whenever I asked questions, Emily would roll her eyes.

"God," she would say, "don't get my mom started."

By July, I had not learned any new words, Emily still had a stomach roll that made her zip-in-the-back-paint-splatter jeans squeeze themselves open, and Mrs. Freedman started locking us out of the house.

"It isn't good for you to be cramped inside all day," she said. "Kids should run and play."

She was stirring a lemonade-flavored packet of Crystal Light into a glass pitcher on the marble counter, feet away from my mom, who was wiping down the baseboards with a wet rag. I had never seen her do this at home. In our apartment, the cleaning was my job.

"What do you do at your house, Dina?" she said. "Surely your mother doesn't let you mope around like an invalid."

My mom pretended not to hear, but I knew she was worried I would say something about Rick and how the two of them argued. I shrugged. Comparing our apartment to the five-bedroom house where the Freedmans lived was like comparing cream of wheat to cheesecake. At my house, I spent my alone time doing chores, lounging around on my mom's bed in her black teddy, and listening to Kiss 104 on her Walkman. I knew the teddy was a gift from my dad because she kept it in the same ladies casuals shoebox with the pictures of them dressed up for prom. One time in third grade when I cried about not having a father, she showed me the picture of him with long hair and big teeth, blue-gray eyes that looked a little bit like mine if I squinted, and told me I did have a father but he wasn't a good man and didn't have anything to do with us. When I asked about him again, she whacked my butt and told me to stop being a brat.

"Mostly I talk to my friends," I said. "Or I read. My mom says I have to get a college scholarship if I want to go."

Mrs. Freedman shifted her gaze between the two of us, nodding slowly, like the possibility of not being able to afford college was a good, sad worry to have. My mom gave me a look. She didn't care if I lied about having friends, but she didn't like me talking about money.

Emily laughed. "*Sweet Valley High* and *Babysitters Club* books don't count," she said. "Don't you ever read something that comes in a hard cover?"

"No."

"You should borrow *Anne of Green Gables*," Mrs. Freedman said. "Emily will give it to you before you leave."

Mrs. Freedman told us to stay in the neighborhood and not to come back before we'd made an effort not to be slugs. Because this was Phoenix, a city where the asphalt never cooled, she slathered us with sunscreen and left the Crystal Light on the back porch. We were sitting on the wooden swing, considering our options, when Sarah came outside and walked to her mailbox. She was wearing a pair of cutoffs and a tank top without a bra underneath. Even from a distance, I could see her slanty cat-eye makeup and her pink, shimmery lipstick.

When we got up and walked to the road, Sarah looked up from the Safeway circular with a rib eye on the front.

"I was thinking about you two," she said. "I have some old clothes if you want them."

"Really?" I said. I was hoping for a pair of jeans with holes in them. Everyone else at school wore ripped jeans over leggings, but my mom said I had another thing coming if I thought she was going to spend money for me to look poor.

"Sure," she said. "It's good stuff, but college is making me fat." She patted her tiny butt, which was round and perky and barely covered by her shorts. "Hang on," she said. "I'll be right back."

Sarah brought out two Nordstrom bags filled with clothes and helped us carry them to the back porch. "Just leave anything you don't want," she said. "I'll take it to Goodwill."

I wanted to go through the clothes immediately, but Emily said I could have them all because they wouldn't fit her anyway.

"Maybe if you had a couple nice things," I said, "you'd want to get skinnier."

Emily leaned down to double knot her shoelaces. "You're an idiot."

"Well, if your mom makes us go outside every day, you'll lose weight."

"My mom's a bitch," Emily said. "I'm going to tell my dad on her."

She said she was going to walk to her dad's office on top of the Southwest Airlines building and tell him her mom was abusing her. "He takes my side every time," she said. "He knows she's not a good mother."

I put my hand on top of the crown of my head, which was already burning up from the sun and pretended she wasn't talking. Emily didn't know anything. When her parents wanted to punish her, they took away the television. When my mom got pissed, she slapped me in the face. If she got mad at Rick, she threw his clothes off the balcony.

"Maybe tomorrow," I said. "It's kind of far." I was wearing turquoise jellies that had once belonged to my cousin, and if we walked the thirty minutes it would take to get to her dad's office, my feet would be killing me.

I wiped my forehead with the sleeve of my T-shirt. "What about Mr. Afternoon?"

"What about him?"

"Well, it's late," I said. "If we go to your dad's office, we won't see him."

She shrugged. "We're going to my dad's office."

She crossed the street and stood with her hand visored above her eyes. In the grass behind her, a crow splashed in the flood irrigation.

"I'm staying here," I said.

"You can't," she said. "You're my guest, and that means you can't be in my yard unless I'm there, too."

I didn't cross the street until she started moving. Emily was not a bad walker. She had a solid stride and strong arms that pumped along when she moved. Mostly the fat part was her stomach. I followed her past rows of wide houses with pebbled porches and grass lawns. In my neighborhood, the apartment buildings were all surrounded by pink gravel and sand lots where people threw beer bottles and cigarette butts, but her neighborhood was all green—even in July.

When we got to the Southwest building, a tall gray tower with mirrored windows, my shirt stuck to my skin, and my eyes fuzzed from the sun. We walked through a revolving door and into the air conditioning. There was a marble floor and two silver elevators with a framed letter board in between them, listing the offices.

"Do they have a water fountain?" I said. "I'm dying."

Emily shrugged. "I changed my mind," she said. "I'm going home."

"I'm too thirsty to go anywhere," I said. "You shouldn't have made me walk this whole way if you aren't even going to talk to your dad."

Emily shrugged. "So find a water fountain. I'm not stopping you."

"Your mom is mean to you," I said, "because she wishes you weren't her kid."

She narrowed her eyes. "You can't use my binoculars anymore," she said. "As soon as we get back, I'm hiding them."

Emily turned and started walking fast. We went the whole way back to her house with ten feet between us, Emily cutting in and out of gravel side streets lined with prickling cacti and numbered trash bins bulging with boxes and broken furniture. My feet kept slipping in my jellies while I tried to keep up. When we got to her street, Mr. Afternoon's white truck was by the mailbox. Emily went through the metal gate and stopped. When I caught up, she tilted her head toward the casita.

"What?" I said.

"Something's wrong," she said, but she kept her jaw set and her eyes squinty so I'd know she was still mad.

I walked past Emily to the stone path between Sarah's house and the pool shed.

She was moaning the way my mom did at night with Rick. I crouched down, and Emily stood beside me.

"What?" she said.

My toes were sweaty and crowded with dust. "It's Sarah," I whispered. "They're doing it."

Sarah's house was kitty-corner to us, feet away, and she was screaming. Through the binoculars, I had seen her mouth open, but I had never heard her before. I figured he was thrusting himself inside of her while he licked her boobs. Or, maybe she was straddling a chair without underwear, which was my favorite thing she did, and he had managed to do it with her through the spokes. I knew that when we went inside to pee, mine would be slippery.

Emily pinched me. "Dina."

I looked up.

"You're gross."

While we waited for my mom to pick me up, Emily worked on a five-hundred-piece puzzle of horses she'd gotten for Christmas, and I lay on her floor, moving my arms and legs against the cool spots like I was making a snow angel. When I got bored, I told her I was sorry for what I'd said about her mom, but she said I was no longer welcome at her house.

"My mom only invited you because your mom's a maid, and she feels sorry for you," she said. "I didn't want to hang out with you in the first place."

"That's not true," I said. My mom wasn't a maid. Maids worked in hotels and hospitals and wore uniforms. My mom was a housekeeper. "Your mom feels sorry for you because you don't have friends."

Emily separated brown puzzle pieces from green ones. "You're a nymphomaniac," she said. "You're just as bad as Sarah. It's why you love her so much."

It was the first new word all summer. I figured it must mean the same as "slut," and Emily was wrong. Sarah wasn't a slut. She could be on MTV. Besides, Emily had been the one to put the binoculars in my hands. She was the one who'd named Mr. Afternoon and who'd spent hours wriggling around on her bed pretending to be Sarah in ecstasy. If anyone was a nymphomaniac, it was Emily.

"Don't look so disappointed," she said. "It's not like you wanted to be friends with me anyway."

When I told my mom that Emily and I had a fight, she asked if it was my fault or Emily's and if I wanted to apologize. When I didn't answer, she said I could stay home as long as I did the list of chores she left for me and didn't bother Rick if he was still sleeping.

When Rick was there, I read *Anne of Green Gables* in my room, and when he wasn't, I put on my mom's teddy and lay in her bed, listening to her Walkman and thinking about Sarah, but I kept getting distracted by Emily and how maybe she was right about me being a nymphomaniac. I was thinking about this on my mom's bed, listening to Madonna on her Walkman, smelling the powdery smell of Sarah's tube top and pressing my hand between my legs when I looked up and saw Rick watching me. I turned off the Walkman and pulled a pillow on top of myself. He was wearing the green polo shirt he wore to work and laughing.

"How old are you, Dina?" he said. "Eleven?"

I nodded. My face was burning. I wondered how long he'd been watching me.

"What do you think about when you do that?" he said.

I shrugged. He had seen my breasts and my privates, but he was still standing there like it was funny. "Are you going to tell my mom?"

He shrugged. "I don't have to."

Rick didn't tell my mom, but when she left for work, he would ask me a million questions about trying on my mom's lingerie and how long I'd been doing it. He wanted to know if I had a crush on somebody or a boyfriend and whether or not this boyfriend had showed me his business. Did I know what an orgasm was and had I had one and was there anything about sex I wanted to know? Because he was a man and my mom wasn't and he knew what boys liked. He said I was a pretty girl, just like my mom, and this meant I needed to be careful not to give myself a bad reputation. I figured he was just trying to make sure I wasn't going to let a boy see me naked, but a week later, when he was still asking me what I liked to imagine when I took my clothes off, I told my mom I wanted to go back to the Freedmans' house.

"Are you sure?" she said. "Because you don't have to. If Emily did something mean to you, you don't have to hang out with her."

I shook my head. "It was my fault," I said. "I want to apologize."

I got my mom to take me to Kmart so I could buy Emily a puzzle of a field of poppies with the birthday money I'd gotten from my grandma. It was nicer than the horse puzzle, but when we brought it by the house, Mrs. Freedman seemed more excited about it than Emily.

"Isn't that nice, Emily?" Mrs. Freedman said, taking the puzzle from me. "Wouldn't you like to say something?"

"Thank you for the puzzle," Emily said without looking at me.

"She bought it herself," my mom said. "With her birthday money."

Underneath Emily's T-shirt, I could see the polka dots of her swimsuit. It was after dinner and she had probably been planning to swim, but Mrs. Freedman told us to come inside. "I have some wine in the fridge," she said. "Why don't you and I have a drink while the girls play?"

Emily rolled her eyes. Upstairs, in her room, she threw the puzzle on the floor and took out a book with a picture of a woman in a puffy dress on the cover. I sat on the floor. The horse puzzle was almost finished.

"My mom's boyfriend accidentally saw my privates," I said. "Now he has a crush on me."

Emily put her book down on the bed and gave me a look like I had told her something really terrible. "Your mom's boyfriend sounds like a pervert," she said. "You have to tell on him."

"I can't," I said. "My mom would kill me." "You could tell my mom," she said. "She'd probably want to adopt you and then paint a picture about what happened."

She stood up and started unwrapping the puzzle I'd brought her and told me that she liked it and that I could start coming over again. She was looking at me the way I looked at the skinny cancer kids every Christmas when our church went caroling at the hospital, but it was better than her being mad and making me spend all day with Rick.

"Did you know that Sarah broke up with her boyfriends?" Emily said. "The redhead found out about Mr. Afternoon, and now they're both gone."

"No more binoculars?" I said.

Emily shook her head. "One of them will come back. I've been planning a stakeout. I was right about Sarah being a nympho, but I still want to know what happens."

For the next two weeks, I did whatever Emily told me to do, and when she complained about her mother, I nodded solemnly and listened. After a while, she seemed to forget our fight. She was too focused on Sarah. In her mind, it was a spy movie and we were getting close.

We could keep an eye on things from the bathroom, Emily said, but when the showdown came, we would go to the pool shed. If we climbed on top of the washer-dryer, there was a little window that looked directly into the casita. There was only space for one of us up there, she said, but we could take turns.

We waited. We prepped our locations. We watched Sarah cry into the phone and pace from the bed to the kitchen, chewing on a pencil. We watched her eat chocolate pudding in her lavender pajamas. Sometimes she left, and we imagined it was to plead with the redhead. Once, we saw her on the street, cleaning her car, but when we asked how she was doing, she said, "Fine, thanks," and wanted to know if we were enjoying the clothes.

We expected the redhead to come by any day and make up with her, but when we heard a car stop and ran to the window, it was Mr. Afternoon, pounding on her door, holding roses and a silver balloon that said, "Be Mine." We shoved our feet into tennis shoes and ran outside. I followed Emily through the porch and the yard, past the swimming pool to the pool shed. It was dark with yellow slats of sunlight on the linoleum. The shed smelled like chlorine and fabric softener. It was hard to breathe.

"You watch," Emily said, gesturing to the washer-dryer. "Just tell me what happens."

"You can watch," I said.

She shook her head. "I'll lift you. You're lighter."

She netted her hands together and boosted up my legs so I could crawl onto the space above the washer-dryer. I had to lie on my stomach and then lean a little to the left without slipping. I could hear the tone of their voices and see the bed and desk through the front window. They had to be behind the door.

Emily reached into a basket of towels and pulled out the binoculars. "Here."

Through the binoculars, I could see a coffee cup by the typewriter and the pair of lavender pajamas she always wore, balled up in the bed. Sarah's socked foot edged into view and then she leaned up against the desk and crossed her arms.

"What's she doing?" Emily said. She was beside me, underneath the window.

"Nothing," I said. "He put the flowers in a vase, and he's giving them to her, but she doesn't look happy."

He set the vase on the desk behind her, curving his arm around like he was going to hug her, but she wriggled away and started pacing.

"She's mad," I said.

"Yeah," Emily said. "I can hear her, I think."

Mr. Afternoon leaned close and said something loud, and she spit on him, right on his face, so he had to let go and wipe it off with his T-shirt, and when she did that, everything changed.

Emily tapped her fingers on my leg. "What's happening? You're not doing a good job of explaining."

He grabbed her arms and pushed her down onto the bed. Her face got red. It looked like she was having trouble breathing. He unzipped her jean shorts and pulled them past her hips and then unzipped his own pants without letting her up. She kept wriggling her shoulders and slapping his arms, but it didn't matter. He was stronger.

"They're fighting still," I said. "She's going to slug him."

Emily squeezed my ankle. "I bet he told the boyfriend," she said. "Mr. Afternoon told the boyfriend, and now Sarah hates him, but she'll come around."

Sarah's shorts were around her knees, and she was still wearing her T-shirt. Except for his naked butt, he was clothed too. I'd seen them have sex a dozen times before, but this was different. I could see the hair on the backs of his legs, the circles of dirt on the bottoms of her socks. What they were doing looked more like a fight.

"I bet she gets back with Mr. Afternoon," Emily said. "I bet you a million trillion dollars they start kissing. Are they kissing?"

"No."

Once he was rocking back and forth against her, she stopped hitting him, but instead of moving into him like she usually did, she just lay there with her hair spread out, staring off like the Iranian woman in Mrs. Freedman's painting. When he squatted down to pick up his pants, I thought she would hit him, but she pulled on her shorts and wrapped her arms around her knees.

"She doesn't like him anymore," I said. "They're broken up now for good."

While he paced in front of her, Sarah sat still and watched him. Her curly hair was flat, and she wasn't wearing any makeup. She looked more like we did than Madonna, and maybe this was who she had been all along—a girl with makeup and hairspray, pretending. I handed Emily the binoculars, and she helped guide me onto the linoleum. There was no point in telling her what had happened. She would just say it was gross or that Sarah was gross and then complain about something her mother had done or why her life was hard.

Emily put the cord around her neck and slipped the binoculars under her T-shirt to hide them. "You're bored with her now, aren't you?" she said. "Now that she's not a slut?"

"Maybe," I said. I followed her out of the shed and into the house, but I was thinking about the way Sarah's face had blanked out: where her mind traveled, what it looked like there, and if it was a place I'd someday go to.

The Fourth Fattest Girl at Cutting Horse Ranch

We've been waiting thirty minutes for Jeanine to get back from the airport and take us on our morning run when the intake van pulls into the gravel lot in front of the big house, lighting the stucco white and red. Jeanine, a triathlete, is the only nurse fast enough to keep up with the anorexics. My roommate, Mien, runs for Stanford and can do three miles in about fifteen minutes. The other girls are slower but still give enough of a shit about running to come to Wickenburg, Arizona, and the only treatment facility in the United States whereupon goal weight, you can run three miles a day. Everywhere else, it's Jazzercise and slow meditative walks. Running can burn nine hundred calories per hour.

Like the other bulimics and binge eaters, I'm on mandated exercise, the difference being I'd come anyway, whereas the fatty binge-eater/bulimics would mean to but wouldn't. I used to exercise a lot, like two hours on the StairMaster followed by an aerobics class, but in the past five weeks that I've been here, I've stopped binging and drinking, and I've dropped from a size twelve to a ten with just twenty-one miles a week. If I stay like this or get thinner, it will almost seem worth it that I had to sell the stocks my grandma left me to transfer out of the hospital in Michigan and pay for this place.

Normally the anorexics would be in total mutiny about the delayed run, but we had a meeting yesterday about patient privacy, and this means the newbie's famous. There are eight of us on the porch, and everybody, even Mien, who's usually too mature and important to involve herself in the drama, is angling for a better look.

"I hope it's not a reality star," she says. "I'm not interested in spending the next two months with somebody desperate for attention."

Amy, a blonde high-schooler, shakes her head. She's tiny, but her face is puffy from weight that hasn't settled. "I bet it's that girl from *Next Top Model*," she says. "Did anybody see those bikini pictures in *People?*"

Bianca, Amy's tagalong ninth-grader, nods. She is fourteen but flat-chested enough to look like a child. "They're giving her a really hard time," she says.

Mien rolls her eyes. "Getting that girl would be good news why exactly?"

Bianca and Amy give each other a look.

The three fatty binge-eater/bulimics have their women's wear sweatpants pressed up against the limestone knee-high wall. They are hoping for a skinny new girl to hate. When a half-dead anorexic arrives so emaciated she can't sit down without a pillow keeping her butt bones from piercing skin, they can say things like, "Show me a man who finds that attractive." According to them, I am good-looking because I have "meat on my bones," which is their way of saying my body is a realistic goal weight for a woman who is a size twenty-two, whereas an anorexic's body just makes them feel bad.

For the anorexics, it's different. When a new girl shivers under her paper gown at weigh-in, her spine jutting out like a rocky garden hose, they are quiet out of respect. The new girl is a memory of what's been lost—a mirage of what it means to be skinny and empty and good.

Me, I'm the nightmare. I'm the warning of what they could turn into if they aren't vigilant. They know better than to let themselves become fat women, but they could get lazy and grow boobs. When they stand with their feet pressed together, their thighs could touch. When I first got here, Bianca and Amy made a list of everyone from fattest to thinnest, and I was number four—just after the binge-eater/bulimics who spend their days waddling around, talking about food.

The driver's side door opens, and Jeanine gets out and waves. "I'm sorry!" she yells. A girl in a blue dress appears. It is hazy out and hard to see much. Jeanine opens the sliding door and helps the girl with a big black suitcase. They walk toward us.

"It isn't her," says Bianca. "Even if she dyed her hair, the model's way thinner."

Amy grabs Bianca's arm. "Jesus. It's freaking Jessa Korteweg, and she's *fat*."

"Who?" I say.

"Um *Terrorist Planet, Lost in Seville*," says Bianca. "She modeled for Versace and Prada for like a decade, and now she's an actress."

I shrug. Bianca smoothes her hair. Jeanine is wearing bicycle shorts that show off thick squares of muscle above her knees. She looks like a man, but the anorexics dig it. They admire her discipline.

"Ladies," she says. "We have a new patient. This is Jessa."

Jessa waves. She has red puffy lips and large blue eyes slanted like the ones you see on sketches of extra-terrestrials. She is not fat or thin, more like swollen but clueless about it, the way frosh girls are at college when the drinking and study food puts heft on an effortlessly lean high school body.

Bianca slides off the ledge and gives Jessa her hand. You can tell it's hard for her not to seem disappointed. "I really like your Prada ads with the puppies and the skyscrapers."

Jessa nods and shakes her hand. "Thank you," she says. "I also like that campaign." When she says "campaign," it's clear she has a foreign accent.

Trish, who is in her midtwenties and gets Boniva injections in her hip every morning for her osteoporosis, unties and double-knots her shoelaces. "We aren't running?" she says. "We're really not going to go?"

Jeanine smiles. "I need to take Jessa through check-in," she says. "She's been traveling for twelve hours."

"We could skip breakfast," Trish says. "That would solve the problem entirely."

Jeanine shakes her head. "Please," she says. "Don't be difficult."

Jessa points to her suitcase. "I have trainers," she says. "I'll go to the jog."

She slips off her ballet flats and pulls her dress over her head. She is wearing nothing except for a black lace thong but doesn't seem self-conscious about her naked butt or her little pink nipples bobbing up and down. Squatted down like that, she has ripples of cellulite on the backs of her legs but is still a perfect curve. She yanks on yoga pants and sits down on the porch steps to tie her shoes, still shirtless. Mien rolls her eyes.

"Thank you," Trish says. "It's just. This is the only exercise we get."

We move to the edge of the property and an empty two-lane road, lined on either side with sand and brush. In the distance, the sun is coming up behind gray-blue mountains. Within minutes, Mien is way out front with the other anorexics struggling to stay close. I can run a mile in nine minutes, which is something considering I got sent to the hospital in Michigan because of abscesses in my lungs from puked up food that got trapped, but beside these girls, that's glacial.

Jessa jogs up beside me. She is running with her arms too straight. "Those girls," she says, out of breath. "They seem—cuckoo."

"Just wait," I say. "Amy put a pat of butter in her hair so she wouldn't have to eat it, and Trish ate a bar of soap to give herself diarrhea."

Jessa makes a face and stops running. "I'm sorry," she says. "I'm not in shape."

I stop running with Jessa at the coyote-crossing sign, which is the halfway mark. I am barely sweating, but Jessa's bra has little dots of moisture between the boobs.

"You don't seem cuckoo," she says.

"You don't seem like a bitch."

"You are surprised?" she says. "Because I am an actress?"

"I am surprised," I say, "because you are at Cutting Horse Ranch. Everybody here is a bitch. It would be easier if we were allowed to drink."

"Oh no," Jessa says. "I have signed up for a prison."

I say this even though drinking is the thing that got me into trouble. Everybody at the Chi-O house would get drunk and do stupid shit, but I would come home and forget myself. I'd spend the whole day eating lean meat and vegetables, and then after four hours of vodka, I'd plow through the kitchen. First it would be macaroni and cheese or pizza with the other girls, but then I'd sneak a package of Oreos into the bathroom, and when I'd eaten so much that my stomach distended, I'd spend the next hour puking. My eyes and nose would be leaking all over the place, my vision flashing with stars, but I didn't stop until I saw bile.

In our room, collecting our things for the shower, Mien closes the door. "What a diva," she says. "Did we really need a five-minute preview of the model's boobs?"

Mien doesn't do naked. When she's changing her clothes, the new outfit goes on before the old outfit comes off. She has a boyfriend, but they haven't had sex. In her mind, nudity is a kind of rudeness.

"Trish was freaking out," I say. "Jessa was changing fast so we could run."

"Come on," she says. "She tied her shoes with her shirt off. She wanted everyone to look at her model/actress tits."

"If I had that body . . . " I say, thinking about Jessa's butt in the black thong, her high round boobs. Mien rolls her eyes.

Jessa spends the rest of the day in new-patient orientation, and when she sits with me at dinner, her eyes are red. We all used our thirty minutes of media time to Google her, and so I know she is Danish and twenty-one. After her mother died in a car accident, she gained twenty pounds, got fired from a movie, and gained fifteen more.

"It gets better," I say. "The orientation is the hard part."

"Does it?" This is Teri, Jessa's roommate, who has long iron-gray hair and a prematurely curved spine from two decades of starvation.

"Yeah," I say. "I think so." What I mean is that there is something nice about routine and food that comes in plastic, measured cups. When I feel bad about myself and want to block it out with food or booze, there's a medical staff to stop me.

Teri takes a bite of an apple. "I'm not an optimist," she says. "But that's what happens when you grow up with Dad's dick in your mouth."

I have heard some variation of this story at least once a day, but Jessa reddens and cuts her steak up into tiny squares. The dining room has a wall of windows and wooden round tables that seat four to five people. We are supposed to focus on the light and on the conversation. Food is supposed to be nothing more than a routine that keeps us healthy, like brushing our teeth or washing our hair. No one ever mentions taste.

"Teri," I say, "we're eating." Teri should get this, but she raises an eyebrow, and I feel myself getting defensive. "That's supposed to mean what?" I say. "I like food?"

"You're awfully sensitive."

Jessa wipes her mouth with a napkin. "I like food," she says. "I'll admit it."

"I didn't think models ate," Teri said. "I heard we got a model, and I figured you'd be a skeleton."

"A lot of the girls are young," Jessa says. "Everyone is skinny when they are young, yeah?" She looks at me to confirm.

This is not my experience, but I nod.

Teri looks around to see if the nurses are watching and then blots the oil from her piece of chicken, shaving, maybe, fifty calories. "You're an actress, too, though, right?" she says. "Maybe it's easier when you aren't just a model."

Later that evening, Teri asks Jessa if she has stretch marks from having gained so much weight, and Jessa requests a room change.

By the next day, we are roommates, Jessa on the bottom bunk, me on the top. Mien is pissed because this means she has to room with Teri, but Mien is always pissed about something, so I don't feel that bad. The first night, I hear Jessa crying and climb down the ladder to sit with her. She moves over to the far side of the bed, and I lie down beside her, making sure to concentrate on my breathing and on the air conditioning so that I am not thinking about the fact of a beautiful woman in tiny cotton jogging shorts, inches away.

"I miss home," she says.

"This is a weird place," I tell her. "But it gets better."

"I miss my family."

She puts her head on my shoulder and snuggles it against my neck. She smells like soap and lavender. "You could go back to Denmark," I say, reluctantly. "I mean, if you really hate it here."

She crawls over me to stand up and produces a British tabloid with a picture of her on a bike with her legs circled in red. The caption says, "*Terrorist Paunch?*"

"If you search my name," she says. "The first suggestion is 'Jessa Korteweg fat.'"

In the afternoons, after snack and before dinner, we lie out by the pool in our swimsuits. Mien joins us in a tank suit covered with running shorts. The other anorexics keep their clothes on, never putting more in the pool than their legs. Jessa has different bikinis she mixes and matches, all of them cut so small you can see her hip bones and butt poking out. She has a round little belly but doesn't seem to care. I wear a one-piece that ties around my neck and a pair of board shorts just big enough to cover the cellulite on my thighs. I know better than to try to look sexy.

"You are funny," Jessa says. "I've never seen girls in such large swimming costumes."

"Swimming costumes?" Mien says.

"I like it," I say. "Like an entire disguise for when you undress."

"You don't like to be naked?" Jessa says. "Not for sex?"

Across from the pool at the glass card table, the anorexics squirm. When Jessa isn't looking, I adjust my lawn chair so the angle between my legs and waist is bigger, which flattens out the bulge that's pushing against my board shorts. "Yeah, well," I say. Mien sits up. She has the body of a child. I mean, she wears size ten in kids and still has to get the pants hemmed. She doesn't have hips or boobs. She does not look like a sexual person.

"You have sex," Jessa says. "Don't you?"

"Yeah," I say. "Sometimes."

"With men?"

I can feel my face burning. The truth is, I have had sex with only three people, and the first two times were with drunk guys I didn't know. I slipped out before morning and walked back to my dorm room in the dark, barefoot, holding my high heels. The third time was with a girl in Chi-O, right before I came here, but it was only once, and she got mad about it after and told everyone I'd molested her.

"My boyfriend wants to have sex," Mien says.

Jessa picks up her hair and winds it into a loop on the top of her head. Her clavicle sticks out and makes a little hollow below her neck. "What are you waiting for?"

Mien shrugs. "I'd like to be married," she says. "Then, you know, if he wants to leave me, it's complicated for him legally."

She has two pictures of this guy above her desk, and he looks like what he is: a math major at Stanford.

"I think he'll probably just be glad to fuck you," I say. "He didn't leave you after you gave him a blowjob."

Mien blushes and narrows her eyes.

"I'm sorry," I say. "It's just, half the time I could have been eating a sandwich and not missed anything."

Jessa sighs. "I don't know," she says. "It depends. I've had sex with loads of men, and it's always different but usually nice."

Does "loads" mean ten men? Thirty? Fifty?

"Maybe it's different for models," I say. "I bet the men bring out their A game."

That night, after lights out, Jessa asks if I'll come down and sleep beside her.

"I want to talk to you," she says. "I need to say something."

I climb down the ladder and lie in her bed. She leans on her arm to face me. Her hair is pulled back with a silk handkerchief, which makes her cheekbones stand out in the grainy light shining through the frosted glass window.

"It's okay with me if you don't like men," she says. "In Denmark, it is different. It is okay. Everyone sleeps with a girl sometimes."

I make myself keep my eyes forward, but I can't swallow. "I'm not, really—"

"It's okay is all," she says and kisses my forehead. "I like you anyway."

I touch the knot of her kerchief. "Your hair looks good like that."

She laughs.

"It does," I say, whispering now, almost breathy. "You can see your face."

She kisses me again, but this time, she kisses my mouth and pulls off her shirt. She breathes against my ear. "Don't be embarrassed," she says. "You are not so bad, you know." She takes off her pants and underwear and straddles me. "Come on."

"The nurses," I say, thinking about the doors here, which don't have locks. About how getting caught would mean going back to the state hospital. "They might come in."

"We'll be quiet," she says. "I promise."

I try to stay as flat as possible so my stomach won't scrunch together, and then she is grazing her nipples along my body and saying how bad she wants to fuck. When my fingers slip inside of her, she lets out a little murmur, and I pull up close against her. She opens my legs with her knee, and my body melds against hers like we're working hard toward something important, and my brain is so dizzy I forget to think how I must look, spread out below her, my whole body visible and open.

Days go by when I don't try on all of my clothes to see if I am getting bigger or smaller. I am not dumb enough to think I am Jessa's girlfriend or that she loves me, but there is something new that happens because of what we do at night. My body is both more settled and more alert. The air seems brighter and easier to breathe. On our morning runs, Jessa stays in bed, but I zip past the red rocks and the droopy, green mesquite trees like a woman on fire. I get faster than Bianca and Amy. Almost as fast as Trish.

The nurses think I am getting well, but the truth is, when I look happy or strong, it is me thinking about Jessa and how she hates everyone here but me. About how on the good nights, she puts her whole hand inside of me, and the next day it hurts and I have proof of what happened, evidence I am not making it up.

One night, when the room is still blurry from sex, and we are lying beside each other, holding hands under the covers, woozy and warm, but clothed now in case the nurses come inside, I tell Jessa I am falling in love with her.

She sighs. "You're not in love with me."

"Yes," I say. "I feel giddy all the time. I feel like I'm on drugs."

"What you feel," she says, "is that you are a lesbian and have just figured it out, but I am not a lesbian, okay? Please don't try to make me a girlfriend."

By the end of June, four weeks before I'm scheduled to move across the street to a step-down unit with its own kitchen, I have still not held Jessa's hand in the daylight or had sex with her without a nurse's station outside the door. This, I decide, is why she doesn't believe that I love her.

"We should get out of here," I start to say casually. "We should plan a trip."

Every day I brainstorm the ways out—pretend family visit, trip to a medical specialist—but Jessa is the one who finds it: a road race in Phoenix on Fourth of July weekend. It should matter that Jessa is not a runner and only starts running again after she pitches the idea, but because she is self-admitted and because she offers to finance the entire trip, we are granted a weekend of quasi-freedom: forty-eight hours at a resort in Phoenix with Mien along for the race and Jeanine as our chaperone.

By late afternoon, we arrive at the resort on South Mountain, a hillside of little gray houses, half-priced for the hot season. Jessa has ordered two suites with a door between them that locks—one for Jeanine and Mien and one for us. We head straight for the pool, a half circle with a flat edge that disappears against the horizon. Behind us is an orange metal gate, scrub trees, a red mountain. Down the hill below the pool is a field of Kelly-green grass, imported from somewhere else. I had expected men to leer at Jessa, and before we've unlocked the gate, three men tense their whole bodies, gawking. I think, *You don't have a clue.*

We drop our towels and bags on an L-shaped couch, and I feel their eyes following us. They are indistinguishable except they are different heights and have different hair colors, all of them muscled and preened and holding their heads high like they can't wait for us to ask what they do for a living. Part of me thinks Jessa will be naive and let these morons flirt with her, but I know I'm paranoid.

Jessa slips off her cotton dress and folds it. She is wearing a blue string bikini I haven't seen before with just enough fabric to cover the midsection of each breast. She has thinned out so her body is now exactly perfect—the muscles of her stomach pushing against the roundness of her belly, the strings on the bottom half of the bikini making slight indentations in her sides. Jeanine strips down to the kind of boxy, athletic bikini that matches the functionality of her neatly stacked muscles. Mien takes off her shirt and her shorts for the first time all summer. I'm wearing board shorts over a tank suit.

One of the men is sitting on the stone edge and the other two are in the pool below them. There are two middle-aged women by the fence, sleeping with sunhats over their faces. Jessa walks to the edge and calls out, "Is it warm?"

"Like a bathtub," says the dark-headed guy sitting on the edge of the pool. I swear he's puffing out his chest. "I had to get out to cool off."

Jessa points her toe and dips her foot into the water, turns and eases backward down the ladder, her butt in the air, her triceps flexing. She sinks and ducks her head.

Mien takes off her ponytail band and lets her hair fall loose around her shoulders. "You don't want to take your shorts off?"

"No."

She turns to take the ladder down into the pool. My suit is high-necked and sturdy; my shorts are double-knotted, and so I can jump into the pool without anything budging. Jessa swims toward the men, and Mien and I follow.

"See?" says the dark-haired guy. "It's warm right?"

"Almost too much," Jessa says. "But nice."

"It's better in a few hours," says a barrel-chested guy with teeth like Chiclets. "It cools down, and you can see the lights of the city."

"We might go downtown tonight," Mien says, her head just barely above the surface. "We're only here for the weekend."

"Well," says the dark-haired guy, "there's a bar here, and the restaurant's world-class. You stay, and you don't have to worry about driving."

"Plus, you get to hang out with Frank," says the third guy who is skinnier and taller than the other two and has thick eyebrows that look sculpted. He is almost pretty.

"That's true," says Frank, unfazed. "You'd get to hang out with me." He stands and puts on a pair of worn-out leather flip-flops. He walks back toward the tile bar, where a woman in a terry-cloth robe is reading a newspaper and returns with a laminated drink menu. "First drink is on me," he says. "Welcome to Phoenix."

They are college friends from ASU who graduated a few years before and are in town for a wedding. Mien and Jeanine order seltzer water with a lime, and Jessa orders a raspberry margarita. Even on weekend release, we are not supposed to drink. Supposedly, impulse control, which is already a problem for the eating-disordered, gets worse with alcohol. Supposedly, alcohol is something we use to block feelings.

Jeanine shrugs. "Get a drink if you want," she says. "Just make sure you girls are ready for the morning."

I order an Amaretto Sour, which is what I always drank before at school, but then as soon as the waitress leaves, I am thinking about the 295 calories and how alcohol slows your metabolism and about how if I drink one drink, I might not stop. Before, I would drink on an empty stomach, my electrolytes already fucked from puking, and one strong drink could make my skin tingle and my head fuzz. This is when I would turn carefree. When I would gossip and flirt. These moments, when everything looked slippery and vague, were the only times I'd let people see me. When the drinks come, Jessa says hers is too sweet, and I take the glass from her. "I'll trade you," I say, even though hers is at least two hundred more calories.

"Most people don't take summer vacations in Phoenix," says the pretty boy.

"We live in Wickenburg," I say. "We're working at a summer camp for adolescent girls. It's a good job, but you have to get out sometimes."

"Sure," says the barrel-chested guy. "I get that."

The pretty boy is watching Mien, and Frank and the barrel-chested guy are watching Jessa.

"I like working with strong, young women," Jeanine says. "It's inspiring."

"It's like a Girl Scout camp?" says Frank. "Like horses and lanyards?"

Mien dips her head back into the water and rings out her hair. "Kind of," she says. "Mostly, it's girls with problems. It's a little exhausting."

"Yeah," says Jessa. "You could say that." She empties her drink, and in an instant, Frank is waving at the bartender for refills. The sky is bright with the last part of the sun, the final surge of it lighting up the mountains and glinting off the miles of glass buildings on the hillsides below us.

"I worked at a group home for retarded kids in high school," says the barrel-chested guy. "It was like eight dollars an hour to clean up shit. I couldn't figure out why my boss loved it, but then he got arrested for getting the retarded kids to give him blowjobs."

"Jesus," Frank says. "What's wrong with you?"

"I just thought of it," he said. "I forgot about it until she mentioned camp."

"Jesus, buddy," says Frank. "You need to work on your small talk."

After my third drink, the lights along the hillside wink on, and my skin flushes with booze. I haven't been drunk since before I got sick.

Pretty boy says he's hungry and suggests we meet them at the restaurant in thirty minutes. "Sixty minutes," Jessa says. "Maybe more. It's just one shower in each room."

Mien tells Jeanine she can have the shower first, and Jeanine pulls herself out of the pool and toward our belongings in one swift movement.

"The four of you don't shower together and sleep together and walk around naked?" Frank says. "You're ruining my fantasy."

"Sure we do," says Jessa. "But it takes longer with all of the sex."

Frank laughs. The barrel-chested guy reddens. Jessa grabs my hand. She pulls my hips toward hers and kisses me. People are watching, Jeanine's back could turn at any moment, and Jessa's tongue is in my mouth. I can't feel my legs. Jessa pulls away and pushes herself out of the pool, slowly. She grabs her towel and bag but doesn't cover herself or adjust the bottom of her bikini that's riding up her butt. She's strutting almost, her head high, her hips snapping from side to side, and I can imagine her on a runway. She opens the heavy metal door that leads up to the lobby and turns to look at Frank. "I will come find you," she says. "Do not worry."

The men say goodbye and grab their things, but Mien lingers. "Let her shower first," she says. "You and I can swim."

I dip underneath the water and take whip kicks to the other side. The chlorine burns my eyes, but I keep them open. The bottom of the pool is edged with tiny round lights. At the deep end, I surface for air, turn on my back and swim long strokes to the other side. The sky is clear, and the first stars are bright. Mien is resting against the ladder with her feet floating out in front of her.

"Jessa's a bitch," she says. "You shouldn't let her use you like that."

"What?" I say. "I don't. It's not—"

"You have hickeys on your neck," she says. "It's not that hard to figure out."

Her face is warm with, not pity exactly, but something you'd feel for a child, like she sees hope and stupidity inside me, and I have to get away from her. I move to the ladder. "Look," I say. "Thanks for your help and everything, but it's not like that."

On the way back to the room, I pass the restaurant's balcony with a candle flickering on each table and a salsa band's trumpet wailing through the air. I'm hungrier than I have been in a long time. It's been hours since I've eaten, and my body is now used to regular meals. Already, one day away from Cutting Horse, and I am thinking about sugar and fat, the rush of filling my body and making it empty. It is like having an orgasm by yourself, not the feeling exactly, but the single-mindedness, the way your attention gathers itself against the world until the moment closes.

Back in our room, it smells like floral shampoo. Jessa has moved the boxy pillows to an oversized couch and taken over the bed with three minidresses, which are laid out on top of the comforter. When I knock on the bathroom door, it opens and Jessa is standing perfectly naked in front of the fogged mirror, drying her hair. I have not seen her in so much light since the first day when she changed into her jogging clothes. I want to kiss the dimples in her lower back, but I'm not sure if I'm allowed to touch her.

"I forgot how good it is to use a razor without a nurse watching," she says.

Her legs are glistening with lotion and look smoother than they ever were at Cutting Horse, where there are no bathtubs and where razors have to be checked out. Her pubic hair is all but gone now—disappeared into a single brown stripe.

"You're really going to sleep with him?" I say.

She shrugs, flips her hair over and sprays it with an expensive-looking hair product in a blue glass bottle. "Why not?" she says. "I haven't had sex in a year."

I get into the shower and yank the curtain shut. My shorts and T-shirt are soaked from my bathing suit, and I'm freezing. Jessa's long hair is all over the tub, which makes me hate her for never thinking about anybody else, but then I'm winding the strands of hair together and wondering if she'll ever put her head on my shoulder again.

Jessa starts up the hair dryer, and I take off my clothes behind the shower curtain and drop them on the floor. I peel off my swimsuit and turn on the shower, and then I realize I am naked in the same room with Jessa and no nurses—that I am finally exactly where I have waited to be. I open the curtain a couple feet and hang the suit on the towel rack above the toilet.

"I can't believe you're doing this," I say. "You don't even know him."

Jessa switches off the hair dryer, sets it on the counter and faces me. Her hair is now dry and fuzzy on top. "I'm not a lesbian," she says. "I'm not your girlfriend."

She turns back to the mirror and swipes a clear space with a towel so she can curl her hair, and my body appears in front me: a silhouette of curving flesh, neither revolting nor beautiful. I have never stood naked in a lighted room with another person before, and I wait for Jessa to notice my body—to say something one way or the other, but she picks up a round brush and starts curling a section of hair. It won't matter if I stand still and watch the steam layer over my hips in the mirror because she is in her own world.

I step back into the shower, the hot water snapping against my cold skin, and I'm telling myself, *Nobody gives a shit about you. You're disgusting. Nobody can love you because you're a fat pervert with no self-control.* It keeps spinning through me, the way it always does—the old familiar heaviness that always found me after the frenzy of eating and purging had cleared into hunger. The feeling that followed the love of a woman who didn't want to be loved by women so much so that she said, "You molested me. You took advantage," and everybody in Chi-O knew she was right. It is what found me in the hospital when I had stopped breathing because I could not stop purging, and the feeling that found me again at Cutting Horse when Amy and Bianca looked at my thighs and whispered to each other, "Kill me if I ever look like that. Just shoot me in the face."

The thoughts get faster and faster until I am remembering every bad and selfish thing I ever did, every rule I made for myself that I couldn't follow, and then, just as the thoughts get frantic, the hair dryer shuts off, the bathroom door clicks shut, and in Jessa's absence, the chanting shifts into a kind of promise. *Nobody gives a shit what you do. Nobody's really watching. They have left you alone, and you are free.*

Common Application with Supplement

1) Concentration interest (first choice): physics

Concentration interest (second choice): applied mathematics

Parents marital status (relative to each other): never married

With whom do you make your permanent home? maternal grandmother

What five words best describe you? inquisitive, intuitive, logical, quiet, miserly

Please respond in 250 characters (roughly 40 words) or fewer to each of the questions below:

2a) What excites you intellectually, *really*?

Calculating the closest stable orbital path of a asteroid circling a black hole.

2b) Think about a disappointment you have experienced. What was your response?

After my mom shot herself, my boyfriend stopped talking to me. I said, "I get it. You want a happy girl." He said, "Actually, I meant to do this a long time ago." My response was to fuck his brother.

2c) Suite-style living—four to six students sharing a set of rooms—may be an integral part of your college experience. What would you contribute to the dynamic of your suite?

I can wake myself up at a given time without an alarm clock. The trick is practice, light sleeping, and a childhood of uncertainty. Imagine a suite with an easily spooked but friendly guard dog.

3) Tell us where you have lived—and for how long—since you were born; whether you've always lived in the same place, or perhaps in a variety of places. (100-word limit)

For sixteen years, I lived with my mother in a small yellow house in Albemarle, NC, where the neighbors parked on the grass, whipped their dogs, and launched fireworks for the celebration of all holidays. Since July, I've been in Winter Haven, FL, with my grandmother who lives in a dark second-story apartment with a screened balcony and a low-hanging roof that blocks the sun. The walls smell like mildew and two decades of nicotine, but now she smokes outside in the parking lot with everybody else. At dusk, the alligators glide along the creek by the laundry room, feeding.

4) Please tell us how you have spent the last two summers (or vacations between school years), including any jobs you have held. (250–650 words)

1. Summer before junior year, I worked at Pablo's Restaurante, a giant green-shingled building in the strip mall off NC-24 that was run by a short muscular white guy named Barry who smiled a lot but always looked tense. He tried to cultivate an air of mystery

about his heritage, which was Polish. The windows were double-tinted and gave the dining room a husky daytime fog I'd seen in strip clubs on television cop shows where young hot girls get murdered. Midafternoon, the place would be lit up with Christmas lights, and every table would have a candle glowing inside a red glass orb.

I worked six lunches every week and sometimes a Sunday or Monday dinner, the worst shifts, assigned to me because I was new and bad at my job. I usually got the food orders right, but I was slow and unfriendly and didn't like bothering the bussers, who were older than me and Spanish-speaking, and so my tables didn't always get chips and salsa. My strong points were conscientiousness and that I was always on time. I did better when I worked with Andy, who had the kind of dopey easygoing personality that made people trust him. If it was busy, he ran my food, and if it wasn't busy, he sidled up to me in the kitchen and asked, in a voice of true intimacy, about my love for Kanye West.

At our high school, the popular girls treated Andy like a mascot—the sweet funny guy they all thought should have a girlfriend but did not want to date. I was pretty much friendless, but I felt superior to him, too, because I was on the honors track of classes and he wasn't and because it was obvious he had a crush on me. Sometimes we shared an employee-discounted enchilada on the back patio or strolled over to Big Lots and fumbled through dusty sunglasses and party hats. Almost everything I said seemed to put him in a good mood.

Then one Sunday afternoon, he pulled me into the walk-in refrigerator and wanted to know if he was crazy or stupid. I was impressed with his persistence but pretended not to know what he was talking about. We were standing by a metal shelf of produce and the yellowing clear plastic strips that separated the refrigerator portion of the walk-in from the freezer. It smelled like cilantro, salad dressing, and the deep fryer oil that always embedded itself in my hair and clothes. I could tell it wearied him not to look at my nipples.

"I like you," he said. "You know that, right? I mean—I really like you."

His lips were pink and wet. His chest bobbed up and down with tight shallow breaths. His turquoise Pablo's Restaurante polo shirt had a smear of daubed-off sour cream under his name tag. I hoped that if I stood still enough he would list all the things he liked.

"I follow you around like a dog," he said.

He'd worked out a speech about the boundaries we would keep as coworkers and how I would have to stop texting him unless it was about switching shifts and even then it might be better to ask someone else.

"Okay," I said. "Is that all?"

"I guess."

Andy was looking at his sneakers—black leather with embossed gold tags printed inside each floppy tongue—and it was clear that he saw our conversation as having come to a close.

"For what it's worth," I said. "I don't think you act like a dog."

"Thanks."

This was when I kissed him, but the part I remember was right before that, when Andy's face took on this dreamy, panicked glow, like I was his wildest fantasy coming true.

2. This past summer I helped my mom move in with her brother so I could leave for Florida. Her finances were not in any kind of order, her house needed repairs before it could be sold, and because her injuries are what you would guess for a person who survives a gunshot to the head, she was useless. We all knew my uncle was motivated by her disability checks and codeine prescriptions, and my guilt about this, along with the anticipation of freedom, gave me the patience to sit on the cement patio with her each night and listen to her try to talk. "Fuck up," she would say, pointing to herself. "Ugly." Her face never moved the way she probably wanted it to, but her eyes were fierce, her self-hatred a spooky, full-force passion.

When I was feeling generous, I would agree that she had done a good job planning her suicide, that the doctors all said a bullet at that angle should have killed her. She also liked to hear about Andy's brother because he had abandoned me the way my father had abandoned her, and because she thought it was her fault that my life had gotten too sad for him to handle. What she didn't like was to think about hurting me and how she couldn't keep herself from doing it.

At first, her ability to speak was even worse than it is now, and she would count on me to listen closely. If I didn't guess right, she was stuck. I didn't have to let her say my father's name or tell me she wished she could die. I could sit there, swatting mosquitos, pretending that I had no idea what words she wanted, and she couldn't say shit. The woman could barely move.

Sometimes I would beg her not to try to kill herself, and she would gurgle out, "Can't," meaning, "Not physically capable," and I would threaten to punch her in the face.

"I swear to fucking God, Mom," I would say, and her eyes would light up, ready for me to hit her.

In August, I moved to Florida and got to know my grandmother, a careful and fastidious woman who works part-time as a teller at Bank of America. In those first weeks, we watched a lot of reality television and talked indirectly about my mother. Once, she left a dog-eared copy of *Codependent No More* on my bed in the guest room, filled with angry insights about my grandfather written in the margins.

5) Why are you drawn to the area(s) of study you indicated in our Member Section, earlier in this application? (150 words)

In quantum mechanics, the laws of physics no longer operate in the same way that they do with what you can see. In object physics, many things are easy and predictable. The largest force operating on these objects is always gravity, and it's not hard to make accurate guesses about their motion. Given a few equations, a high school sophomore can chart the arc of a football or the highest possible weight supported by the Golden Gate Bridge, but at the size of the atom and the size of the universe, the unknowns multiply. It's impossible to know both the current location of an electron as well as its velocity. It's impossible to see a black hole and currently impossible to explain the origin and purpose of dark matter. And yet—somehow, in these invisible areas of the universe, mathematical equations still predict a lot about how things work.

6) Describe a place or environment where you are perfectly content. What do you do or experience there, and why is it meaningful to you? (250–650 words)

Andy's family lived in a brick and clapboard house on the west side of town, a couple streets away from where the real estate developers cleared out a big stretch of woods to build a new subdivision. The houses came in seven different models. This was a big part of what the billboards promised, along with the fact that you could get to the easternmost edge of Charlotte in forty-five minutes, which, of course, was a lie.

That summer, about half the lots were empty churned-up red clay, waiting for somebody to special-order a house, and the other half were somewhere between the foundation and the finished product. A few of the houses had families in them already who all seemed to have stern young fathers in their driveways, looking around for new neighbors. Most of these people had little kids and minivans that had seen better days, and you got the feeling that they were first-time homeowners. They were doing better than my mom, I guess, but they made me sad. I could see that these were cheaply built homes scattered across a mucky corner of land that always smelled like car exhaust and sulfur rot from the paper mill, and I knew already that their new neighbors would be like the old neighbors who had woken them up with their domestic disputes and who didn't always have money to fix a leaky drainpipe or a broken window.

Usually, Andy and I just walked around the neighborhood, holding hands and talking about nothing, but then other times, we'd duck into one of the unfinished homes to smoke the pot he bought from one of the dishwashers. I guess this was trespassing, but we never touched anything or left nubs of joints or even nosed around very much, we just lay there on the plywood with the nails and sawdust and the unidentifiable bits of plastic junk. I liked to have a house with a second floor and the cutout of where a window was going to go so I could look at the pink sunset and the daylight draining away against the pine frames. In these moments, it didn't matter that I wasn't falling in love with Andy the way he kept saying he was falling in love with me.

I was careful not to say lovey-dovey things I would regret later, but I was less strict with myself about the physical stuff, which I understood to be its own force. In the daylight, I was always scolding myself for noticing Andy's gangling neck instead of his kindness, his lisp instead of his soft eyes, but in the darkness, everything was simple motion. I was a semi-truck wheeling along the highway, a machine without brakes careening through the night.

7) Please briefly elaborate on one of your extracurricular activities or work experiences that was particularly meaningful to you. (100–250 words)

These days Pablo's has two stars on Yelp: one star less than the fine citizens of Albemarle gave the incubated hotdogs at Quik-Trip, but most of the reviews came from an older lady who got fired. Carla was a horrible waitress, most definitely stealing from tip out, probably on drugs, but she'd been fucking Barry for years. Then he got another girlfriend in addition to the wife, and her bad waitressing was noticed. This was an unassuming woman who had, for whatever reason, loved Barry, but now she wanted him to suffer. She made up stories about rat meat in the albondigas soup, maggots in the ice machine. She said, maybe this was true, that Barry was missing a testicle. One night, she drove over to Pablo's, slashed Barry's tires, and then banged on the office window, screaming about what a motherfucker Barry was, what a goddamned motherfucking one-balled liar. There were a bunch of us in the office, and I could tell that everybody else thought this was funny, but Carla scared the shit out of me. Until that night, I had thought of her as someone who knew that disappointment was inevitable and had taught herself to bear it.

8) Why This School in Particular? (200–word limit)

In my dreams of college, I am always at the front of a classroom, solving a math problem so complicated that sound fades and I forget where I am except for the numbers. I haven't faced any problems this hard yet because the better of my two high schools only goes up to Calc. I and AP Physics. At your school, there are research labs that test nuclear fission and galaxies and scholarships to study abroad in the southern hemisphere and spend a semester looking through a world-famous telescope. There are also thousands of students who come to your school from the kind of communities where kids are taught to expect good things to happen to them, and I think I would like this a lot.

9) Recount an incident or time when you experienced failure. How did it affect you and what lessons did you learn? (250–650 words)

In the weeks before my mom shot herself, she was displaying all the classic warning signs. Namely, she was giving away her possessions, and the gloom that had clung to her for the past several months was lifting. She had been working through some changes in her medications, but most of her depression that winter was the same kind as usual—a guy had dumped her and now she hated herself.

When my mom was at her worst, she exercised twice a day and replaced her meals with the protein bars and muscle milk she got from Gold's Gym, where she worked at the front desk. Her body went gaunt and bony, and she spent a lot of time in the bathroom emitting bad smells. Her other depression activities included watching action movies, curating playlists of 1990s punk songs for her workouts, and sleeping.

That winter, when I was not at track practice, studying with my friend Regina, or working at Pablo's, I was at Andy's house, doing whatever Andy was doing that day. Officially, we were not dating, but this was just my way of letting him know not to count on me. I figured I wasn't leading him on since I was honest about my feelings and had given him my virginity, but Andy, who is an optimist by nature and slow at hearing bad news, saw things differently.

My mom started cooking dinner again in March, and by April, she was taking me to the movies once a week, which she could not afford to do, and we were having long talks about the good things my teachers said about me and how she wanted my future to be different than hers. One day, she said, "If something were ever to happen," and I said, "Don't—okay? Please don't."

Then she went on about this emerald ring from her great aunt that I was supposed to hide from the bill collectors. The other thing I had to promise was that I'd move in with my grandmother, who had been a bitch to my mom but good to me, and that I wouldn't move in with my uncle, who has a drug problem and an evangelical wife.

I knew what she was telling me, but I also thought, "Maybe this is a fantasy." Maybe this is like getting yourself to sit through the antibullying assembly by reminding yourself you can pull the fire alarm.

Still, when my mom said that she thought it would be a good idea to put her car in my name, I called the guy who'd prescribed the antidepressants. I could tell he thought I was right to worry but also that he was more concerned with doctor-patient confidentiality and liability. The phone call lasted about four minutes.

I also called the ex-boyfriend, who said my mother was a kind but troubled woman and that he wished her the best. He did not seem to think he owed anything to a woman he'd dated for two years, and this kind of attitude, I suppose, is how he manages to own a Mercedes. I used to drive over to his house on the way home from the hospital and stare at his perfect floodlit yard, wondering what it would do to him if I threw a rock through his window. Would he even know who did it?

To sum up, I learned that 1. Knowing the future can't always change it.

2. Tragedy looks inevitable when enough people refuse to help.

10) Describe a problem you've solved or a problem you'd like to solve. Explain its significance to you and what steps you took or could be taken to identify a solution.

According to Andy, he has a good memory about the two of us, and my memory is bad. He can recall specific conversations and quote back promises I've made. For instance, in October, apparently, I told him that I would be ready to revisit the issue of dating in December. Then December came, and I'd forgotten about all of this, and so when he tried to be my boyfriend, I wouldn't hang out with him for a week. According to Andy, I did this on at least six separate occasions, and, whether or not I meant to, it was a way of teaching him never to ask for anything. He said that if a guy did this back-and-forth business to a girl, he would be an asshole.

According to Andy, he said he loved me four times, and I only ever said it once, kind of, after he forced me. It was a January afternoon, overcast, and we were on opposite sides of his computer room—me by the window in this unsteady papasan chair that felt like it would fall apart if I moved too much, and him pacing back and forth along the wall. His parents were out for the night, his brother was playing video games in the den, but instead of having sex, we were talking. Andy said it didn't bother him that other people thought he was pathetic but that he needed to know I cared about him, too.

"Okay," I told him. "I care about you." I was tearing up the way I always did at the first sign of tension between us, but I was angry. It didn't seem fair that Andy got to use his love as proof that he was a good person when all it really meant was that he was a guy who knew what he wanted.

"But do you?" he said.

"Do you want to stop seeing each other?" I was only a couple feet away from this glass-eyed taxidermy fox that Andy was proud of having purchased himself from the Goodwill in High Point. Its tail reminded me of a dust mop coated in dog hair.

"That's your answer to everything."

I squinted at him. I couldn't explain why, if I didn't love him, it felt unbearable to let him leave. I figured it had something to do with my mother—the way I had lived my whole life toggling between the fear that she would abandon me and the fear of being crushed by how much she needed me—but I also knew that this was my fault. I was a small-hearted person who wanted to be loved completely without having to give anything in return. It felt safe this way, and I was pretty sure it was how I would always feel.

"I do love you, Andy," I said, kicking a wool sock against the carpet. "But it's with the love of a small and stingy heart."

Saying this made me feel wise and stupid at the same time.

I said, "You shouldn't wait around for me to change."

I was sure that I would lose him. But Andy loved me back then, and, for a little while, this was enough.

11) We all exist within communities or groups of various sizes, origins, and purposes; pick one and tell us why it is important to you, and how it has shaped you. (250–650 words)

I grew up in a family of two. My mother was a small woman with wavy brown hair, blue eyes webbed with white, and porcelain skin that bruised easily. I understood from a very young age that it was my responsibility to keep her safe. When I was little, I would beg to sleep in her bed so that I could watch her in the night and make sure that she kept breathing.

She liked stock car racing and loud music with electric guitars. She often wore her hair looped up with a pencil. She drank so much Diet Coke that her front teeth lost their enamel. She did not go to college, and this embarrassed her if it ever came up. Men loved her, and she needed their attention too much to ever tell them no. Every time a man wanted her, it felt like a surprise and a cure—the thing that would finally sustain her.

When I was in middle school, I broke up with two of her boyfriends, a skinny guy with a red beard that glinted in the winter sun and a beefy old man who threatened to kill her.

"She doesn't want you," I told them both, through the screen door. "Now you have to go away or I call the police."

The bearded guy stayed there for a long time, sobbing, but the beefy guy calmed down when I explained that there was no other guy in my mom's life.

My mom shot herself at nine o'clock in the morning, while I was at school. She did it outside on the back patio, where, she has told me many times, it would be easy for somebody to hose off the blood. She wanted someone who wasn't me to find her and then clean up her mess, which was mostly what happened, except that the neighbor found a living person with her face exploded, screaming, and the blood stain on the cement is still there.

When I saw her in the hospital, she apologized for doing such a bad job at killing herself and said that she had hoped I would think it was an accident. This was why there had been no note.

"An accident?" I said. "How is getting shot in the head going to look like an accident?"

She didn't have an answer to that, but I could see that she was sincere, and so I shut up. In health class, Mrs. Sheehan said that scientists have found fetal cells in the bodies of women who were pregnant many years ago and that the cells can heal things. We were supposed to feel some big poetry about the connectivity between us all—the way it's confusing where one person starts and another person ends—but just about everybody in the class threatened to puke. They didn't want to think about their moms' bodies, and they definitely didn't want to imagine parts of themselves lurking around in their moms' organs. I was the only one who thought this was so obvious that it wasn't worth talking about. If my mother was in pain, I felt it; if she needed a part of me to heal herself, it was my job to help.

12) In this essay, please reflect on something you would like us to know about you that we might not learn from the rest of your application, or on something about which you would like to say more.

On the day that my mom shot herself, Andy and I had been on a break for almost a month. When I called to tell him, he was upset with me for making contact.

"Okay," I said. "But it's an emergency."

"I'm not your boyfriend. You've made it pretty clear this is what you want."

I waited on the line for a minute. It sounded like Andy was driving.

"What is it?" he said, finally, and so I told him.

It is true that he came to check on me, and it is also true that he helped me figure out some logistical issues with the hospital and with school, but this was all done with an attitude of pity and obligation. He no longer wanted me.

As a joke, I said, "It's been so long you must have a new girl now," and as it turned out, he did. I had seen them hanging around at school together—a popular girl with shiny blond hair, perfect teeth, a laugh like a wind chime. I'd figured that he liked her but never considered for one second that she would date him.

"What did you expect?" he said. "You want me to pine over you forever?"

"No," I said, though, of course, this was exactly what I wanted—that no matter what went bad in my life, I would have this one person who longed for me.

The next day, I went over to Andy's house with the excuse of returning a lasagna pan to his mother and the intention of breaking up his relationship, but he wasn't home. His brother, Jordan, said he would probably be gone for a long time. Jordan and Andy were Irish twins, but Jordan seemed a lot younger. He was skinny, quiet, less good at making friends. They both had freckles and small rounded ears that stuck out like barnacles. The effect was worse on Jordan, who wore his hair in a buzz cut.

"He's with her, isn't he?" I said and wrinkled my nose. "Emma."

"Probably," he said. "I'm sorry."

He'd answered the door in mesh gym shorts and a racing sweatshirt from Dupont. His face was flushed, and I had the distinct feeling that I had interrupted him masturbating.

I shrugged. "I'll get over it."

It was April, and a loop of crocuses was blooming around an oak tree in their front yard. It was breezy, but I was sweating. I'd worn my tightest jeans and a burgundy turtleneck that Andy called my "sex shirt" because of how big it made my boobs look, and I could see Jordan noticing my efforts and feeling sorry for me.

"How's your mom?" he asked.

"Not dead."

"That's good, right?"

"Yeah."

Rocco, the lab that I had walked many times with Andy, was wagging his tail and trying to get past Jordan's legs so that I could pet him.

"Do you want to play on the Wii?"

I nodded.

The Wii was in the den, along with the washing machine and the old couch where Andy and I lounged around, watching movies and making out, but I walked right past the den and up the stairs toward Jordan's room, kicked off my Converse sneakers, and sat on his bed. It was the only room in the house that I hadn't paid attention to, and I was surprised that it was so neat and so empty. Aside from the furniture, the only decorations were two photographs of him and his friends at the beach that he'd printed out on typing paper with a color printer and taped to the wall.

"What are you doing?"

"Don't ruin it," I said. "If we talk about it, it won't happen."

He shut the door behind him and walked toward me. "This is about Andy, right?" he said. "You want to make him jealous."

He didn't sound mad at me so much as confused. He could tell that there was a larger plan at work but couldn't make sense of it.

"I don't think so," I said, truthfully. "I think I just feel lonely."

He nodded as if he accepted this rationale and walked around the bed to sit beside me. We started kissing, and then I took off my shirt, and the rest was easy. He was nice. I waited for the blank moment where my mind wandered away from my body and then scrubbed itself clean, but the moment didn't come. I stayed exactly where I was, staring at the blurred photographs of Jordan's friends and the oval sunspots gliding across the low popcorn ceiling. I was a seventeen-year-old girl whose father was long gone and whose mother was probably going to be paralyzed forever. I had been loved once by someone who had given up on me, and now I was on my own.

A strained but empty feeling came over me—like the sensation of being lost in a familiar neighborhood, trying hard to remember something that should be easy. I thought about that night at Pablo's when Carla slashed Barry's tires and then banged on the door like a psycho while everybody laughed and about my mom's ex-boyfriend in his fancy house, hoping he never had to talk to her again. I thought about the black holes I'd read about that were too small for anybody to ever know they were there, and I thought about how if I told my mom what I did with Andy's brother, she would be proud of me. She would be glad that I was stronger than she was, that I didn't need a man in my life to prove that I existed, and she would be proud of herself, too, for raising me.

I was thinking about her in a judgmental way, but I understood, too, that she was right: she had raised me to take care of myself, to survive on my own once she was gone. In some small bright corner of my mother's brain, this was the thing she wanted. I wasn't ready to imagine myself shaking loose of her, but it was the first time I realized that I could. There was another life out there for me, a tiny pinprick of light in the distance, waiting.

What
Counts
as Love

When the swelling went down, and she could almost see straight again, Karleen got a job as a carpenter's assistant at Mint Hill Construction, sweeping up debris and helping the skilled laborers with whatever they needed. The job site in east Charlotte was a midrange condo development sandwiched between a wooded neighborhood of narrow houses and an empty parking lot with a faded banner that promised a Target Shopping Center was coming soon. Two condos were finished and several others framed, but most of the site was composed of large, flattened-out mounds of red clay marked with wooden stakes.

It was not far from the duplex where she'd been staying with her sister, Mandy, and her husband, David, sleeping on an air mattress in the small yellow room that would soon belong to their baby. Her sister's neighborhood was just forty minutes away from the lake house she'd shared with JT, but it might as well have been a different universe. Instead of boats and water skis, tires, rental signs, and rusty disemboweled cars cluttered the lawns.

On her first day, she parked on the street behind a mud-splattered pickup truck, waited twenty minutes until exactly five before six, and then walked across the red clay to the aluminum trailer, where Abe had told her to meet him. The air was cold against her bare arms, but she knew she'd soon be sweating. Three Hispanic men stood by the side of the trailer, talking in Spanish and holding large plastic thermoses that looked more like buckets. When she passed them, their eyes watched her walk up the steps, knock on the door, and slip inside.

Abe was wearing a navy-blue Mint Hill Construction shirt with his name on a patch. His long gray ponytail was sectioned off with multicolored rubber bands. She'd never met him before, but like everybody else at the church she went to with Mandy and David, he'd seen her name on the prayer list and wanted to help. He shook her hand a little too hard and gestured to a metal folding chair across from a particleboard workstation holding an old desktop computer and a large plastic tub of Winn-Dixie brand Cheetos. He copied down her driver's license number and told her to bring a photocopy of it and her social security card. Then he went over the safety procedures, which he said included not just the hard hat and goggles but the good sense to pay attention all the time, no matter what.

He led her across the clay lot and past the men in tank tops and frayed jeans congregating in the garage of one of the finished condos, which was filled with lumber and power tools. He showed her a rusted wheelbarrow, a large metal dustpan and a broom with thick bristles curved into an L.

"Don't take too much at once," he said. "You'll want to at first, but you'll be working a long day, and you'll tire out."

By the time the sun had come up, the workers had divided into crews and were spread out across the site. As soon as she swept up one building and hauled the load to the dumpster, the floor of the next was covered with nails, screws, and plastic water bottles. No one bothered with trashcans or bags, but the floors had to stay clean so the men who walked around on metal drywall stilts, which looked like a combination between crutches and pogo sticks, didn't trip.

By eight o'clock and the first break, she had sunscreen in her eyes and a U of sweat around her sports bra. The space between her shoulder blades ached, and the meat of her palms was pink and sore. A young roofer with quad muscles so thick she could see them through his jeans came over to the trailer where she was leaning into the shade and trying to avoid a conversation. He handed her a half-frozen bottle of Gatorade.

"You don't stay hydrated, your legs will lock up on you," he said, in a Kentucky accent. "It's a long day out here, and it only gets hotter."

Karleen took the bottle and swallowed a sip of sweet-salt slush.

"I'm Avery," he said, winking. "Probably I saved your life." He continued, "I mean, that's worth one date at least. Don't you think?"

She crossed her arms so he wouldn't see her nipples under her sweaty shirt. "No."

Avery shrugged. "I'll give you time to get to know me," he said. "Women love me. You'll see."

Karleen laughed. "I'll bet."

Avery licked his cloudy teeth, which were pink with Gatorade. "A summer romance for a summer job," he said. "Isn't that how it works?"

May was not yet over, and she hadn't thought past the end of the week, let alone the end of the summer, but she found herself shaking her head. "This isn't for the summer," she said. "This is my job now."

"You better learn something other than cleanup, then," he said. "The crew gets real small after summer when the work slows down."

Karleen was twenty. Outside of the year at Taco Bell when she was seventeen, she had never had a job. She'd thought she might become a hairdresser after high school, but then she'd met JT, who said he didn't see why she needed a job in addition to taking care of him, which was hard enough. He was twenty-four and the youth group leader at the church where she'd grown up. The other kids liked him because he could imitate the way Pastor Anderson's face shook when he preached and because he brought in posters and tickets from TriStar Motorsports, where he did marketing, but Karleen was drawn to his vulnerability. She saw the flicker of sadness that always flashed across his face after a joke, and this is how she knew he needed her.

She'd had sex with her junior-year prom date the year before she'd met JT, but JT wouldn't sleep with her until she turned eighteen and was old enough for them to get married at the courthouse. He told her she was a born-again virgin now that she was taking church and God seriously and that their wedding night would be the real first time she had sex.

For the first few months, JT complimented the recipes she taught herself from *Bon Appétit* and the way the granite counters and hardwood floors gleamed. When they argued, the issue was always her high school friends and whether she was keeping up with them so she could talk to the prom date. So she hid her prom pictures at Mandy's house and saw her friends only in the afternoons when he was at the office. One Sunday, she wore her hair up in a barrette for church, and when Pastor Anderson shook her hand at the door, he told her she looked beautiful.

JT was silent in the car, but when they got home he said, "How long have you been screwing him?"

Karleen poked him in the chest and laughed. "You're jealous of a sixty-year-old?" she said. "That's pathetic."

His face was red, and she knew exactly how pissed off he was, but she didn't stop.

"If I were going to screw somebody," she said, "it would be the choir director, because he's hot."

And that's when JT punched her in the ribs and left a disk of swollen tissue just above her lungs.

After work, Karleen found Abe on the far side of the dirt lot, loading his tools into the back of his truck. On the window of the cab was a bumper sticker with a picture of a revolver that said, "I Don't Dial 911."

"I have a big favor to ask," she said.

He looked at her fingers, which were worrying a blister.

"You aren't quitting on me, are you?" He squinted at her but kept his eyes warm, and she wondered what all he knew. Behind him, the framers were moving the lumber back to the garage, where it could be locked up for the night. One of them had the same buzzed hair and bowlegged strut as a friend of JT's she'd met once at a bar. She couldn't be sure if he was the same guy, but the sight of him made the blood drain from her face.

"If I could learn to frame," she said. "I'd be able to work year-round, right?"

Most of the men were shirtless or down to a sweat-soaked wife-beater, but Abe still had on his work shirt.

"I'm good with directions," she said. "And I have tools." She was thinking of the starter toolkit she had spent the weekend assembling from second-hand stores and garage sales. She could hear the eagerness in her own voice, and it made her cheeks burn.

Abe pushed his fingers through the scruff on his chin. "You wouldn't rather do office work in the long run?" he said. "Something'll open up at the warehouse if you're patient."

She shook her head and made herself keep his gaze until he looked down at the bed of his truck.

"Okay," he said finally. "You start coming in an hour early off the clock, and I'll get you started."

In the mornings, with the streetlights still on and the sky starting to pink, she helped him inventory the day's materials. He showed her how to cut studs and calculate the pitch of a roof, stood beside her, guiding her hands as she made looping cuts with a coping saw. At night, after work, Karleen read *Blueprint Reading for the Construction Trades*, a dog-eared manual from the 1960s she'd picked up at the public library, and quizzed herself on terms like "common American Bond" and "queen post."

Her body began to toughen—her forearm muscles fattening, her back broadening, thick calluses forming where the blisters had healed. She'd thought the saws would scare her, but she liked the way the vibrations shivered through her arms and legs, the way her heart picked up when the blade began to whir. If she wasn't careful, she could slice her hand open, and the rush of this focus—her mind still and quiet against the spray of sawdust—thrilled her.

At the police station, she asked Shanda, the victim's advocate, what would happen to JT, and she shrugged. She was a big woman in a clingy nylon dress who always seemed tired and out of breath. The last time Karleen had seen JT, he'd broken the orbital bone on the left side of her face. She'd had surgery to remove the bone fragments from her eye socket, but her left eye was slightly lower than her right, and when she looked directly above her, the world went double. JT had been charged with strangulation and serious injury, but he was out on bail, a release conditional upon his keeping the terms of the restraining order she'd filed against him.

"Could be probation," Shanda said. "Could be a couple years in prison."

The room was empty except for a police academy calendar and a poster of a dusty purple peony in a black plastic frame. Like all the police officers and social workers Karleen had encountered, Shanda had constructed an office that wouldn't give any clues about who she was.

Karleen swallowed. "He tried to kill me."

"I'm with you," Shanda said, "I am, but if he gets probation, you might be safer." With probation, she explained, JT would live close by but would have three years of monitoring and could practice fighting the urge to come hurt her, knowing if he did, he'd go back to prison. "Prison is different," she said. "With prison, he sits in there a couple years, thinking about how much he wants to kill you, and then they set him free."

Karleen massaged the tightness forming between her shoulders. "Will he go to trial?" she said, wondering if he still hated her and what it would be like to see him.

Shanda tapped a teal green fingernail on the desk. "Let's hope not."

In the afternoons, when David was still at the auto shop, Karleen and Mandy drank coffee and shared articles from the *Charlotte Observer*. Karleen kept it light—mocking the stupid questions people sent to Billy Graham, like, "Is it in God's plan for me to cheat on my husband?" or, "Is my child misbehaving because he is possessed?" But Mandy liked reading from the crime news so she could say things like, "Being in the church won't keep you away from evil, but it puts you close to God, and being close to him is the only thing that helps anyone."

Because she'd met JT in church, Karleen knew Mandy worried she'd given up on God and religion, but Mandy had it wrong. Karleen needed forgiveness now more than ever. The fact that her eyesight was probably damaged forever or that she had a jagged half-moon scar on her ribs was not just proof of JT's cruelty, but also a testament to Karleen's guilt—a memory of what the two of them had counted as love.

Many things she would never tell her sister. For instance, Karleen had often provoked JT on purpose. He'd always given her a warning that he would hurt her, always said, "You stop it Karleen," or, "If you don't back off, I'm going to lose it," but she still said whatever she thought would hurt him most, the exchange she made for the punch he'd land on her stomach, where the black bruise could stay hidden. He'd apologize, telling her, "I love you too much. Thinking about losing you makes me crazy," and they'd cling to each other like accident victims and have the kind of sex that made the whole room spin.

The second to last fight, the day before he stomped on her face, he told her that no one else would put up with someone like her, that no one else in the world could love her, and so she drank with a friend and went home with a stranger. She had meant this to be a private rebellion, but when she came home the next morning, JT was waiting for her in the living room, with her blue cashmere sweater poised on his lap between her pinking shears.

"Did letting some asshole fuck you make you feel like hot shit," he said, his old complaint that had never been true until now. He cut off a sleeve of her sweater and let it rest on the leg of his boxers. "You think he knows your name? You think he gives a fuck what your face looks like?"

His face was puffy and red, and the room smelled like cigarettes, but he was sober. He sat at the coffee table, covered in a collection of fast food wrappers, put his hand down his boxers and started touching himself. He stared her down, willing her to watch him, and in that moment in the dirty living room with blue fabric strewn across his lap and a concerted effort between his eyebrows, he seemed pathetic and childish, a person who deserved to be hurt.

"You know," she said. "I *did* have fun last night. He had a big dick, and I had a good orgasm, and we might have dinner next weekend."

In July, Abe invited her to work on a Habitat for Humanity project he was overseeing for an AME Zion church, whose volunteers wore hot-pink T-shirts that said "FBI" on the front and "Firm Believer in Christ" on the back. The build site was located in an industrial part of west Charlotte, across the street from a body shop with a spray-painted mural of a man dancing with his legs bent at awkward angles. The words "Dirty South" were painted at the top of the mural. Overhead, they could hear low-flying planes leaving the airport. Mandy and David came to support Karleen and the work she was doing—David by lifting and hammering and Mandy by smiling at Karleen from a folding chair on the edge of the lawn, far enough away so that a stray board or nail could not hurt the baby.

At the first fifteen-minute break, Abe spread out a blanket on the bed of his truck so David and Karleen could sit down.

"We sure do appreciate all you're doing for Karleen," David said. "I'm glad she's got somebody looking out for her."

The truck was parked between a culvert and a highway, and the air smelled like car exhaust and swamp.

"Karleen looks out for herself," Abe said.

David rapped his knuckles against the back window of the cab, where Abe had put a shiny new sticker that read "Driver Carries Only $20 Worth of Ammunition." "Well, you're good at the intimidation anyhow," David said to Abe. "I wouldn't try to mess with you."

She could feel her cheeks burning. David had a way of talking to people that sounded complimentary but wasn't. "The sign isn't just for show," Karleen said. "I've seen him shoot rats on-site."

When the time came to stand in a circle, hold hands, and pray, she stood beside Abe. His hand was rough and warm, and she could feel herself inching closer. She couldn't say what she felt, except that she liked standing beside him.

She came to work early on Monday, leaving her house with the street still pitch-dark and the streetlights still glowing, and found Abe in the trailer, checking e-mail.

"Thank you for Saturday," she said. "I never installed floor-boards before."

He swiveled his chair around toward her. He wasn't smiling, but his eyes were bright. He told her she was a quick study and could come back the next week to learn about drywall.

"You're nice to help me," she said. "Maybe I could take you to dinner as a thank-you. I have a two-for-one coupon to Mama Ricotta's on Kings."

He turned back to the computer screen, saved the e-mail he'd been writing and minimized the window. The trailer was chilly, and he was wearing a knit cardigan with large oblong buttons, the type of garment somebody would spend months knitting. She pulled a loose thread from the hem of her jeans and put it in her pocket. The back of Abe's neck was mottled with sunburn.

"That doesn't . . ." she said. "I mean . . ."

He nodded. "Yes," he said. "You name the day."

"Friday," she said. "Friday at six."

That afternoon, she meant to talk to Shanda about Abe and how making friends with him might be a good thing she was doing for herself, but it might also be dangerous. She didn't trust her judgment. The sight of Abe's thin, sun-spotted hands, or the careful way he held a jigsaw, made her want to spend time with him, but the thought of what might happen if the two of them were alone scared her. She had been raised to understand that the worst kind of woman was the one who flirted with a man she didn't want to sleep with, let him do things for her because of his attraction, and she knew that if Abe wanted to sleep with her, she couldn't tell him no.

What she said to Shanda was, "I do not have good sense about men. JT used to send me e-mails saying the only way out was if he killed me, and I still stayed."

Shanda perked up. "You have them?"

"What?" she said. "The e-mails?"

Shanda nodded. Her weave was growing out, and her hair fuzzed at the roots.

"Sure," Karleen said. "He sent e-mails like that all the time." Shanda's face was sympathetic but also focused on the larger plan. She'd thought of something. "You get me those e-mails," Shanda said, "and we can serve him with new charges within the week. An e-mail like that, an actual death threat, that's rare."

That week, the framer who looked like JT's friend brought a grill, hot dogs, and a battery-operated radio, which was tuned to the local hip-hop station. Avery, who was bouncing his shoulders to the music, pointed to a bucket that was on the ground beside the other roofers. Karleen turned it over and sat down. Her soda was lukewarm and her sandwich was damp with condensation.

"You don't eat meat?" said a light-skinned black guy with freckles on the bridge of his nose.

"I didn't bring any," she said. "I brought a sandwich."

"Hey Mike!" he called. "Get this girl a hot dog."

She looked at her boots.

Mike turned. "We don't have hotdogs for snitches," he said.

The guy with freckles laughed. "Come on," he said. "You should always feed a good-looking woman."

Mike shook his head. "Not this one," he said. "I know who you are, Karleen."

"Drama," Avery said.

Karleen left her sandwich on the overturned bucket and walked over to the grill. Her heart was racing. "Listen, Mike," she said. "JT doesn't need to know where I am."

She thought about pulling up her shirt to show him her scar, but she didn't want him looking at her body. "He might be your 'bro' or whatever," she said, "but he's not a good guy."

"You think JT's interested in you?" he said. "He isn't."

She moved closer, so he could see her face. "You aren't going to tell him."

"Drop it," he said. "Nobody cares where you are."

That night she couldn't sleep. David and Mandy were having sex. Mostly, David just breathed loudly, but her sister squealed and shouted, "Keep doing it exactly like that!" and, "Baby, I love you so much!"

Mandy had told her that sex in the second trimester was the

best she'd ever had. "It's a thing," she said. "It's in the pregnancy books. It's an issue of blood flow."

In the afternoons when David was still at work, Mandy liked to tell her about sex toys and positions. Mandy seemed to want Karleen to understand that being a Christian and being married to the only man you'd ever slept with didn't mean you had to be boring, but Mandy's stories always struck her as sweet. David might tie Mandy up with handcuffs, but Karleen could hear him giggling with her and telling her she was beautiful. Toward the end with JT, sex was only punishment or apology. Often, if she told him he was hurting her, he got excited and hurt her more, and so she lay as still as possible and kept her mouth shut until it was over.

On Friday morning before work, Karleen tried on her wicker high heels and the cotton sundress she'd worn to her high school graduation and stood in front of the full-length mirror in the hallway. It was tighter on her butt and back than it had been before, and now it was too sexy.

"Wow," Mandy said. "You look pretty."

"Did I wake you up?"

Mandy shook her head and leaned against the wall behind her. She was wearing pajamas with yellow moons and stars against a navy background. "You have a date."

Karleen blushed. "No," she said. "Definitely not."

All day, she worried about whether Abe would kiss her. Sweeping up drywall, she found herself imagining that he would try to feel her up on the car ride home, and almost knocked someone off his stilts before she snapped out of it. At shift's end, she lingered with cleanup and then, after they'd put the company tools, goggles, and lumber in the trailer, she followed Abe to his truck.

"Can we meet at the restaurant?"

He opened the passenger's door and got inside. "I'll look forward to it," he said. "Six o'clock, right?"

He started the engine, and the radio came on with a country song about a porch and a girl. He was waiting for her to walk to her car and get it started, and she wondered how her butt looked in her jeans and if her boots made her seem to be strutting, and then she saw a white truck idling on the corner behind a crepe myrtle. She knew before she saw him that JT had found her. She started running. Abe's truck was twenty feet away. Her heart was pounding, and she couldn't think straight.

"Abe," she said, "help me."

"Huh?"

"There's a white truck on the corner that belongs to my ex. He wants to hurt me."

Abe told her to get inside the passenger's seat and lock the door.

"He's not supposed to come within a hundred feet of me," she said. "He's not supposed to know where I am."

"This is the one you got away from?"

She nodded. "I have scars," she said. "I'll show you." She lifted her shirt.

He kept his eyes in the rearview mirror. "I believe you," he said. "It's okay."

"Just look, please." She pulled up the edge of her bra so he could see the shiny white swirl of skin that ran along her ribs. She wanted him to know.

Abe shook his head. His neck was red, and he was breathing hard. "You're safe now," he said. "He won't hurt you again."

He left the engine running but put the car in park. He reached across her and took a pistol and a box of rounds from the glove compartment.

"What are you going to do?" she said.

"You get down real low," he said. "Crawl down onto the floor if you can fit."

"Abe."

"You're okay," he said.

She pushed the seat back and lowered herself onto the floor mat with her knees up against her chest. In the side mirror, she could see the white truck speeding over the clay toward them. She took out her cell phone and called Shanda, but her cell went to voicemail.

When JT got out of the car, Abe was standing across from him with his pistol cocked.

"Is this a standoff?" JT said. "I'm here to talk to Karleen about a legal matter."

"You aren't talking to her about anything," Abe said. "You need to leave."

"And you are?" JT said. "You are who, exactly?"

She knew JT and how he was. He didn't do well with people telling him what to do. He'd get himself killed before he would listen.

"I'm not leaving," JT said. "Karleen is my wife." Then, calling out, he said, "Karleen? I know I hurt you. I'm sorry, Karleen. Can you come out here? Can we talk?"

"Come on, now," Abe said. "You've done enough to that girl. You leave her be."

She moved her head up a little. JT was wearing a suit and holding a bouquet of roses. He was thinner than usual, and his hair had grown out. He turned in her direction. "I see you," he called out, walking toward her. "You've got to talk to me Karleen," he said. "You can't throw around charges like attempted murder and then hide."

Karleen opened the truck door and let her legs slide out in front of her. They felt loose and numb. She hadn't seen JT since he'd been on top of her, stomping on her, since she'd had to play dead until he left the room. "I'm not hiding," she said, her voice braver than she felt. "I just don't want to see you."

They were in a triangle now, the three of them, nobody more than ten feet from anybody else. In the distance, across the street and behind the trees, the traffic on the highway was whirring past.

"You almost killed me," she said. "My eyes don't move right anymore."

JT shook his head and swallowed hard like he was trying not to choke. His face had a funny expression on it as if he'd suddenly forgotten where he was. "I didn't want you to leave me."

"You hurt me," Karleen said. "You put me in the hospital."

He came toward her, close enough that she could see the sweat on his forehead. "I wasn't the only one," he said. "You know what you did."

Abe held the pistol in the air and fired a warning shot as loud as fireworks. "Stop while you're ahead."

JT kept walking. "You don't know her," he said. JT was in front of her now, with his arms open like he was going to hug or tackle her.

"This is it," Abe said. "Stop moving."

"JT," Karleen said, "please."

"We're going to talk," he said. "That's what I came for, and I'm not leaving—"

A second shot rang out, and JT crumpled. His hand was pressed against his chest. Karleen stood over him. "Oh my God," she said. "Oh shit. JT."

"He won't die over it," Abe said, his pistol still out in front of him. "I got his shoulder. You want at him?" He gestured to the pistol.

She shook her head but found herself moving closer. JT's eyes were blinking with pain, and he was moaning. Curled up, he looked small. His face was pinched and red, and his jacket was covered in blood.

"So you're fucking this guy?" JT said. "Is that it?"

She meant to kick him once in the ribs so he would know what it felt like to have the wind knocked out of him, but then her boot made contact, and she couldn't stop. Something inside her had snapped, and she wanted to break him.

"I'm not who you came for," she said. "I'm different now."

"Jesus, Karly," he said. "Come on."

His hands were covering his face and his knees pulled into his chest, trying to avoid her blows. He sounded like a child, pleading. She could walk away. He'd broken the terms of his bail and would go to prison. He'd come for her in the first place because he was desperate, because she finally had the evidence to put him in prison. She knew that, but she also knew the bones of the body, the tiny spaces that would hurt forever if you hit the right spot with just enough force.

A
Real
Marriage

She met Amir in May at the Friendly Market convenience store, where he worked and where she was buying Miller Lite with her roommates, and by July she asked him to marry her. His travel visa had expired two years before, and now INS wanted to send him back to Morocco. Supposedly this had nothing to do with the fact that he was young, male, and Muslim, but Abigail was suspicious, and she liked the idea that marrying her boyfriend could help combat discrimination. Besides, Amir was the only person who had been remotely interested in taking her virginity, and she was twenty-one years old. Letting him leave the country could only be a mistake.

"It doesn't have to be a real marriage," she said. "We don't have to tell anyone outside of the judge or whoever it is that does it, but if we got married, you could stay."

"I don't know," he said. "That doesn't sound right."

"It doesn't have to sound right," she said. "It has to sound practical."

They were sitting on the duct-taped leather couch in his apartment, watching *Judge Judy* and enjoying their last hour alone before Amir's Palestinian roommate, Rayed, would come home. Rayed was nice enough, but he made Abigail uncomfortable. When he wasn't cooking a greasy lamb dish and crooning along to Arabic music, he was staring at her boobs and asking her why more American girls weren't good like she was.

"We need to take care with this decision," Amir said.

She shrugged. Her heart was racing. From the beginning, she had suspected that she liked Amir more than he liked her, but she was hoping he wouldn't notice. "I'm offering to marry you. If you don't want to marry me, just say so."

Abigail would graduate in August. She had finished the course work for her communications degree but hadn't yet passed the swim test required by UNC for graduation. She had already failed it twice. This time, she was taking a swimming class. Her mother, who worked at the post office in Hickory, had told her to use the last semester wisely before she wound up working a crap job with an idiot boss, but Abigail couldn't figure out what type of job she wanted, let alone how she might qualify herself to get it. She had majored in communications because she thought taking classes with cheerful people who wore Easter-egg-colored sweaters might make her friendlier, but it hadn't worked. Surrounding herself with the optimistic just made her more anxious and depressed.

The only time she felt something close to happiness was with her new roommates, whose spare room she was subletting for the summer—three willowy philosophy majors who spent most of their time smoking pot and watching TV ironically. Unlike her mother and her college friends, who had all graduated and moved away, the philosophy majors seemed to think she was doing just fine. She had lost her virginity—they'd taped her underwear to the fridge with a Post-it on the crotch that said, "De-virginized!"—

and she was learning to swim. "One thing at a time," they said. "You don't want a corporate job anyway."

Before the week was up, Amir called and told her they could get married, but only if she took it seriously.

"This is what my mother thinks," he said. "I agree also. Marriage should not be convenient."

"Marriage should not just be convenient," Abigail said. "Besides, your mother married a stranger when she was fifteen."

"Yes," Amir said. "My mother, who has been married for thirty-four years."

Whenever Amir talked about his family, it made Abigail feel proud of him and also jealous. His biggest dream was to return to Marrakech with years of savings and make everyone's life easier. Abigail had a six-year-old half-brother she barely knew, had never met her father, and couldn't spend more than four hours with her mother unless they were both drunk.

"Thursday's fine," she said. "I know you're off most of the day, and I'm free after twelve thirty."

"This would be forever," Amir said. "We would live together and make our lives go in one direction."

"I get that," Abigail said. "I know what marriage means."

They each needed a witness for the ceremony. Amir asked Rayed, and Abigail asked Courtney, the friendliest of the philosophers, a tall blond with a tattoo of Escher's staircase on her back, a girl who was auditing Swimming for Beginners just to keep her company. The morning of the wedding, Courtney left a Post-it on the fridge that said, "I picked up a shift at the co-op. I need the money, and weddings aren't my thing."

When Abigail called the other two philosophers, they said they didn't want to encourage a bad decision. While fucking a Muslim had been very cool and counterculture, marrying him betrayed a lack of understanding about feminism. In the end, Amir called a Saudi friend from his night job.

For their honeymoon, they drove to Carolina Beach and stayed in a half-empty hotel with peeling aqua-blue railings and a sign out front that said, "GOD BLESS, 56 NIGHTLY." The hotel had a kitchenette with pots and pans and dishes, but mostly they ate sandwiches and olives, and Abigail drank wine. She almost never threw up or had a hangover, but she knew deep down that drinking made her happier than most things. Drinking combined with other things she liked, such as sex or cuddling or chocolate cake, was even better.

For two days, they watched television and had sex, and Abigail tried not to think about her roommates. Amir said she had family now that she was married, and would therefore never be abandoned, but this didn't make her feel better. She barely knew him.

On Monday morning, when she arrived at the aquatics center, Courtney was on a bench out front with two cups of coffee from the co-op, waiting for her like always.

"Your head isn't covered, and I can see your elbows," she said. "Does your husband know?"

Abigail reached into her bag for her student ID. "That's not funny."

Courtney stood up. "It's a little funny," she said. "You picked him up at the gas station."

"He has a college degree," she said. "He speaks three languages. He's not some moron."

That day in swim class, they worked on breathing in the shallow end. Everyone had a partner and a kickboard. One person held on to one end of the kickboard and walked backward, while the other person used the opposite end as a landing dock. There were eight of them in the class—each uniquely pathetic. One girl wore a faded Hawaiian-print bikini that invariably showed at least one nipple, and her tall kickboard partner had "F.B.G.M." tattooed in block letters on his upper arm, which he freely admitted meant "Fuck bitches. Get money." These were the other people who had reached adulthood without learning to swim, and it made Abigail think she and her mother were probably trashier than she'd guessed.

On her way back to Amir's apartment, she called her mother at the post office. "You forgot to teach me how to swim," she said.

In the background, there was a shrill beeping signal like a truck reversing. "You sound funny, Abby," her mother said. "I can take a smoke break and call you on my cell."

Her mother had stopped smoking three years before, but she still stood outside with a lit cigarette every hour to clear her head.

When Abigail pointed out that hourly doses of secondhand smoke weren't great for your lungs either, her mother always started in about how hard it was to raise a kid by yourself. Usually her mother was talking about BJ, the pale, allergy-prone child from her latest marriage, but if she thought Abigail wasn't appreciating her enough, the kid her mother had raised alone was her.

"Well, I got married," Abigail said.

She could hear her mother breathing, but she didn't say anything.

"He's a Muslim," Abigail continued. "But he likes me a lot, and he probably isn't using me for my connection to the US Postal Service."

"What?"

"He doesn't seem even vaguely interested in letter bombs or anthrax," Abigail said. "In fact, the first time I asked him to marry me, he said no."

Her mother said she'd call back after work, but she didn't.

After some initial research at the public library, it became clear that Abigail and Amir would need to live together for the marriage to count toward his immigration status. This meant they could have sex without a listening audience and that Abigail would not have to put up with the philosophers' knowing looks whenever she cooked dinner for Amir or washed his laundry. But they didn't have any furniture, and their only money was Amir's savings for his family. Abigail needed a job.

At first, Amir said he wanted her to concentrate on her schooling—that he would simply get a third job doing whatever most Americans were too lazy to do—but when Abigail explained that she had lots of time and that if she worked at Friendly Market, they might actually get to see each other occasionally, he agreed on the condition that she never work alone at night.

Friendly Market was owned by Rayed's uncle, Hassan, who was older and married, but, like Rayed, wore too-small jeans and had yellow-gray teeth crowding his mouth. When he offered her a job, he asked if they were going to have a baby.

"Probably," Abigail said. "Having babies is the only good reason for marriage."

She had hoped he would nod in agreement to give her something to mock him about later when she was in bed with Amir, but instead he looked confused and explained how to secretly notify the police in case of a robbery.

By August, Amir had successfully completed his first immigration interview, and though he would have to pay back taxes and fees, it seemed he would get to stay in the country. They were observing Ramadan, which meant waking before sunrise to eat dates and drink water and keeping the hours of sun free from food. At night, they could have sex, but because it was considered unclean, they had to wash themselves before the sun came up. Abigail liked the drama of living this secret life in the dark, but she could also see how being hungry for thirty days a year could get old.

During the second week of Ramadan, Abigail made the mistake of talking about fasting, and Courtney stopped showing up to swim class just when they were about to move into the deep end. Abigail had to partner with the swim instructor, who insisted she put her face in the water and practice lifting her mouth to either side. When she finally made it to the far end of the pool, clutching the kickboard and the instructor, Abigail was out of breath and shaking too hard to get out of the water.

"I don't think you're actually breathing," the woman said. "I mean, you're lifting your head and everything, but I don't think you're actually taking in the air."

Abigail nodded. Her head was spinning, and she couldn't stop thinking that at any moment her fingers would slip and she would be at the bottom of the pool, dead. It was the feeling of standing on a bridge and leaning too far, but it was a hard thing to explain to people who'd spent their whole lives swimming.

Abigail worked at Friendly Market three nights a week. Because Amir was almost always working at the warehouse, it was usually Rayed who sat with her. She liked having someone around, but not him. He wore too much cologne and seemed to spend a lot of time thinking about how slutty American women were.

"American women are very different," he would say. "In Palestine, women do not go to dance clubs or kiss strangers."

"Most women don't do that here either," she said and tried to decide if this was true. She had kissed a stranger once at a party, but this was mostly because the people she did know didn't want to kiss her.

"Yes," Rayed said. "But in Palestine, all of the women are good."

In her second week, Courtney and the other philosophers came in and bought a pack of cigarettes and a case of Miller Lite. When she paid, Courtney looked at Rayed and gave Abigail a tight hug.

"If you ever decide to leave the Moroccan, we have room for you," she whispered. "Just say the word."

When they left. Rayed said, "I like your blond friend."

"Courtney has a boyfriend."

Rayed shrugged and his eyes lit up with the same expression she'd seen on his face at a dance club when he was grinding against a drunk college girl. "Maybe soon she won't have a boyfriend," he said, and she knew he was imagining Courtney naked.

On Saturday morning, Abigail's mother called to say she had the day free and could drive to see her. "You're living with a man," she said. "And I'm your mother. We should meet."

Abigail hesitated. It would be easier to have dinner together in a couple weeks when Ramadan was over, but Amir was waving his hands in the background and nodding.

"Yes," he was whispering. "We'll cook dinner here. Tell her to come for as many days as she wants."

When she hung up the phone, he scolded her for not immediately welcoming her mother into their home. "Family is important," he said. "Family is the most important thing."

"So I gather."

A day didn't go by when he wasn't calling one of his family members or telling her how excited he was to see them again and bring her with him. Without really talking about it, they'd both imagined an eventual move to Morocco, and to Abigail's surprise, this made her happy. She liked the idea of living in a compound surrounded by dozens of relatives. Not knowing a common language would give her a kind of anonymity. She would spend the whole day smiling and cooking with the women, and when Amir came home from his job, she would speak.

Amir was doing exercises in the living room. Every day, for fifteen minutes, he did sit-ups, push-ups, and calisthenics. The body, he liked to say, did not need to run a marathon, but it did like to be moved.

Abigail always said, "I hope that's a very bad translation of something wise," and usually this made him laugh.

Now, watching the twitch of his triceps, she said, "My mom is very American."

Amir exhaled and held his arms straight. "It doesn't matter about your mother," he said. "You are my wife. By the law, you are a person I like."

Her mother arrived in the late afternoon and announced she needed to pee. She was wearing a plush red sweat suit and carrying a large black purse with a giant medallion that said, "GUESS."

"I'm sorry, honey," she said. "I really am glad to meet your boyfriend, but I can't hold it."

She had dyed her dark hair a yellow blond that made her skin look sallow, and it was cut into a short, stacked bob. "Abby, honey," she said. "Move it."

When Abigail heard the bathroom door close, she squeezed Amir's hand. "See?"

"You didn't tell her we're married?" he whispered.

Abigail nodded. "She knows we're married. She calls you my boyfriend to be a bitch."

Amir winced. "Baby," he said, "be nice."

He brought the box of dates to the living room and set them on the crate from Friendly Market they were using as a coffee table. When Abigail's mother returned from the bathroom, he asked if she would prefer water or milk.

"Vodka," she said and nodded toward her purse. "And I'm Stephanie. I'm where she gets it. I'm Abby's crazy mom."

"We also have orange juice and coconut water," Amir said. "Or I can go to the market."

Her mother laughed. "I tell you what," she said. "If you have children, you should do it exactly at age thirty. Eighteen is too young, and thirty-five will kick your ass."

"I can go buy wine," Abigail said. "I don't mind."

Abigail could sense the way the apartment must look through her mother's eyes. Secondhand furniture, clocks with Arabic letters in gold. A framed engraving of a passage from the Koran.

Her mother sat down on a folding chair beside the card table in the kitchen, almost knocking her head on the hanging brass lamp. "I really do have vodka in my purse," she said. "I wasn't kidding you."

Abigail took the vodka from her mother and made two screwdrivers. Drinking would break both the daily fast and her informal agreement with Amir that they would abstain from alcohol during Ramadan, but she was not used to being with her mother without alcohol. It was one of the few things they had in common.

"I'm sorry, sweet pea," her mother said. "I don't mean to walk in here bitching, but BJ has been a little shit all afternoon."

"BJ's here?" Abigail said.

"Well," her mother said. "He's sleeping, finally. He's pissed at me because I wouldn't let him go dirt biking with his cousins today."

Amir sat down at the table. "BJ is your son?"

"He's sleeping," her mother said.

Abigail and Amir carried BJ up from the car and let him sleep in their bedroom until it was time to eat. He was allergic to milk, wheat, carrots, apples, and chocolate, but he could eat the lamb Amir had made. Her mother didn't seem concerned. When she began explaining the plot of Sally Field's *Not Without My Daughter* to Amir, Abigail poured more vodka into her orange juice.

"I thought you weren't drinking," Amir said.

"I wasn't," she said. "I didn't mean to."

"Is she in trouble?" her mother said.

"Please stop," said Abigail.

"Okay," her mother said. "I'm just saying."

"It's only for a month," Amir said. "It's Ramadan."

"Well, we're Christian," her mother said. "Abigail is Christian."

Abigail took a sip of her drink. In spite of the fact that Amir was angry with her, she was beginning to feel blank and relaxed. It was nice having her mother say the things she couldn't.

"Abby wanted to celebrate with me," Amir said. "It was her choice to observe the fast."

Abigail and her mother each had two screwdrivers, and when they moved to the living room, she let her mother braid her hair and tell stories about how shy and strange she had been as a child.

"This one, too," her mother said, nodding toward BJ, who was making his Power Ranger dolls jump off the couch. He grinned up at her, knowing he was being talked about.

When the vodka was gone, Abigail asked Amir to drive them to Friendly Market. She knew she'd be hung over in the morning if she didn't stop drinking, but she wanted to hold on to the feeling she had, the closest she'd come to calm since leaving the philosophers and moving in with Amir.

In front of the store, a squad car was parked sideways across two spaces, its lights flashing. The store's doors were propped open, fluorescent light spilling out into the parking lot, and a police officer stood in front of the counter, talking to Rayed. Abigail, her mother, and BJ waited in the car while Amir went inside. When he came back ten minutes later, he was holding a box of wine and a coloring book. The store had been robbed, he said, but they had lost less than one hundred dollars. Most of the money had been in the safe.

"You know these people?" Abigail's mother asked.

"We work here," Abigail said. "I told you that."

Back at the apartment, Abigail's mother and Amir agreed that Abigail should not be working at a place that had just gotten held up, BJ sprawled on the kitchen floor with his new coloring book, and Abigail drank a mug of wine quickly enough that her fingers started to feel numb.

"I can't believe this is my daughter's life," her mom kept saying. "I can't believe it, Abby. You are my daughter, and this is how you live."

Later that night when she tried to lie close to Amir, he rolled over. They had given their bed to BJ and her mother and were sleeping on a blanket in the living room. "I'm sorry," she whispered. "I told you ahead of time what my mom is like."

A beam of light from the parking lot made white-blue shadows on the walls. "I'm not upset with her," Amir said. "You're really drunk."

"I'm not like my mother," she said, moving her mouth carefully to avoid slurring. "I'm not like Courtney, and I'm not a club-girl slut. Before I met you, I was a virgin."

Outside she could hear the neighbor's terrier barking and the neighbor yelling for it to hurry up and shit. She couldn't see

Amir's face well enough to know if he was surprised. He lay still for a minute, breathing long, even breaths, and when he spoke, his voice was steady. He asked if she would give up alcohol, if she could if she had to, if she imagined there was a day in the future when she would want to stop. She thought of the stepfathers and boyfriends who had pleaded with her mother before they had all, one by one, left.

The thought of Amir leaving her had somehow not entered her mind as a real possibility before, and though she had known him only a few months, thinking about separating from him made her dizzy and breathless with panic.

"I'm a good person," Abigail said. "I only drink for fun," but she could hear the quiver in her voice, and if she were Amir, she wouldn't have believed her either.

Two days later, she failed her swim test. Everyone else in the class passed—even the girl with the sunflower tattoo who had to doggy-paddle—but when it was Abigail's turn, she choked, and the instructor had to jump into the pool and help her. The instructor let her stay after and try once more while she swam beside her, but Abigail couldn't stop shaking.

When Amir came home, he found her in the bathtub, crying. "You don't like being married," he said. "Do you?"

She shook her head. "Turn around," she said. "Stay in the room but don't look at me."

"I have seen it all, you know," he said.

"Turn around."

"I'm your husband."

He handed her the pink towel that was sitting on the lid of the toilet, but instead of getting up, Abigail pulled it into the tub with her and tucked it around her body. "I failed my swim test," she said. "I have to come back in the fall."

He moved the shower curtain against the wall and sat on the edge of the tub. "It isn't fair," she said, but she knew that wasn't true. Everyone else in the class had passed the test. She had failed because she didn't take responsibility for her own life. It was the way her mother approached the world—drunk and bitter, waiting on somebody else to show her how to be a person.

Amir took off his shirt and pants and got into the water behind her, still wearing his boxers. He put his arms around her, and she leaned back against him, the wet towel covering her like a blanket.

"Next time, I will sit on the side of the pool watching, and if you think you're going to struggle, you look to me."

He smoothed her hair and kissed the top of her head. "We will get a private lesson," he said. "I will help you. I will be there."

Abigail closed her eyes and tried to see her life with Amir the way he saw it. He would sacrifice and provide for her on principle. Not because he loved or understood her, but because he had decided that someday he would.

"I love you," she said slowly, trying on the words, wondering how much time would have to pass before they'd be true.

The
Next Thing
That
Happens

After dinner, my mom pulled me into her bedroom, shut the door, and sat on the edge of the king-sized bed with her hands in her lap, fidgeting. I leaned back against the cool of the comforter and told her, okay, I was listening.

I gave my sister Alyssa a black eye yesterday, along with a line of teeth marks on her shoulder, and so I'd figured out what my mom would say. I've been in two fights at school this year—one with Nicole, the girl who used to be my best friend, and one with a high school girl named Christina Horner who slammed my head against the locker and made my nose bleed all over my dress. My mom said the same thing both times—don't fight. Then, she grounded me.

Tonight, she said, "I can't take it anymore, Sally. I just can't."

I rolled onto my side to look at her, but she was busy pulling at the loose skin around her fingernails.

"What?" I said and pushed myself up, which made a sharp pain fly through my right wrist—the one I'd used to punch my sister, and the one I probably broke earlier this year when I fought Christina Horner.

"Your sister's eye was almost swollen shut this morning," my mom said. "And you can't pull knives on people."

I sat on the edge of the bed, hunched over, trying not to be sick. My socks had a brown lawn of dirt on the bottoms—half from the wooden floors in our house no one sweeps and half from tiptoeing on the cold cement in front of our house while I took my dog to the bathroom.

"The knife," I said, "was a joke."

"I called your uncle last night," my mom said. She stopped for a minute, and I knew without looking she was biting strands of skin off her fingers. "He's got a friend in Utah who runs a group home."

That was two hours ago, and my mom expects me to pack up and disappear tomorrow morning. My dad's working second shift tonight at the steel mill, four o'clock until midnight, and he won't be home until after I'm asleep, and unless he wakes up early to say goodbye I just won't see him for a few months. That's how important it is to everyone that I'm leaving.

I tell my mom I want to say goodbye to Nicole down the street and take my bike to the gas station instead. Nicole was my best friend for three years, though it was more like having a twin. Nicole and Sally, Sally and Nicole. We ate together, slept over at each other's houses, swapped clothes. If people saw one of us without the other, they got confused. Even teachers. Then, we got to seventh grade, which is in the same building as the high school, and suddenly Nicole could only see people who were older than us. Suddenly I was babyish and embarrassing, and my secrets were things she could use to entertain her new friends. That's when I punched her, and now she won't talk to me.

Citgo's only about a five-minute bike ride away, but it's on Highway 66, the one busy road in all of Leechburg Township. The highway's one lane on each side with gritty, sloping shoulders that make my tires slip. I ride up by the white line where it's flat, pedaling fast enough to feel my heart pumping away under my turtleneck. The cars whip by, and one of them beeps right behind my bike, and I lose my balance and swerve. For a second, I think I'll crash into the guardrail and crack my head.

When I get to Citgo, Jimmy's pumping gas into a minivan, and he raises his hand toward me and smiles. Usually I only come here in the afternoons when it's slow and boring for him, and when my parents are at work, and even then not too often. He's not my boyfriend, and so I'm careful to give him space.

I lean my bike against the side of the gas station by the woods and wait for Jimmy in front of the garage. He's at the driver's window now, talking to a chubby old woman in a Steelers sweatshirt, waiting to hand her the clipboard with the credit card slip on it for her to sign, but she keeps talking. Everyone likes Jimmy, even old people who wouldn't normally like a boy with shoulder-length hair and a neck tattoo. My dad calls him a nice kid every time we leave this gas station, and he tells Jimmy that he should come work at Allegheny Ludlum after he graduates. My dad would call him something different, though, if he knew what Jimmy and me do together.

The woman reaches for the clipboard, and I know Jimmy's saying, "If I could just get your John Hancock on that," like he always does, talking like an old person.

Jimmy's sixteen and in tenth grade, and I just turned twelve over the summer, but he's nice about it. He says I have what you call an old soul.

He swaggers over with his hands in his jeans, bouncing almost because he knows I like him. He's wearing a red jacket with grease on the sleeve and has his hair pushed through the back of a Penguins ball cap. The cap is for Mr. Gorely who teases him about his hair but wants to take care of him, like everybody, because Jimmy is sweet and has a loony tunes mother and a dad who's a drunk. Mr. Gorely's own kids live over in Vandergrift with his ex-wife, and he lives alone, right here, in a room above the gas station.

"Hey, Sal," Jimmy says, and gives me a side-hug with the clipboard still in his hand. He smells like gasoline, and his coat feels cold.

"Your face is pink," he says and touches my cheek with the back of his hand. After a second he moves his hand away, but my face stays hot. His hands are rough with grease stuck in the calluses and under his nails from working on cars with Mr. Gorely. I told him how my mom makes my dad soak his hands in paint thinner, but he won't try it. I think he likes to have the grease there as proof that he does something real after school, that he's learning a trade, that Mr. Gorely trusts him.

With cars, Jimmy knows what he's doing. Yesterday, an old man came in with a kitchen fork stuck in his tire, and Jimmy jacked up the car and took off the tire and then he put it in a tub of water and started making white chalk marks on the places where the air came out.

Right away he called the man over to him and said, "The fork's not the big deal here. The problem was after the tire got flat and you had to drive here, your rim cut up the inner liner, and the body cord's shot. Look at the sidewall—see?"

The man came over—this old guy, old enough to be my grandfather, but he nods along to what Jimmy's telling him, doesn't argue once when he says the tire's too burned out and torn up to patch.

I was on a folding chair in the corner, looking at my pre-algebra book and pretending not to care how smart Jimmy sounded. It's embarrassing, sometimes, the way I feel about him.

Jimmy looks up above the garage at the yellow apartment that's Mr. Gorely's and says he has another half hour before he can leave. I wonder if Mr. Gorely's up there now, watching us, and if he thinks I'm Jimmy's girlfriend.

"Come on," Jimmy says, and we go inside.

The store part of the gas station is the size of a bathroom—a refrigerator and freezer along the back, one row of candy and gum, another of potato chips and newspapers, and there's the cash register counter with the cigarettes and the chewing tobacco and the wooden stool where Jimmy always sits. The floor is a deep yellow linoleum, the color of runny egg yolks, but it's old and cracked and always smeared with mud.

Jimmy sets the clipboard on the counter and kisses me, slow, with his hands on my shoulders, and then he takes his hat off and pulls his hair into a neater ponytail and hangs the yellow and pink credit card slips on a nail by the counter, just above the deer jerky Mr. Gorely cured himself.

"So what's up, Sal?" he says from behind the counter. "You bust out of your house or something?"

He opens the cash drawer and starts facing the dollar bills in the same direction. He doesn't seem mad that I'm here, just confused.

I shrug. "My mom's making me go to Utah tomorrow," I say. "I wanted to tell you bye."

"Utah?"

I nod.

"I never been there," he says. "Is it pretty?"

I play with the stack of gum in front of the counter, moving the packs from side to side so that the empty slots in the rows change places.

"They aren't going," I say. "Just me. I'm in trouble."

He pulls a cardboard box of money out from under the counter and counts it, moving his lips and squinting his eyes. I don't say anything because I don't want to make him lose count, and because I'm not sure what to say exactly. I want Jimmy to know where I'm going and that I'll be gone for a while, because honestly, he's the only one who might miss me, except maybe for Mr. Gorely who calls me "Love" and gives me free pop. He doesn't count though, because he doesn't know anything bad about me. He just likes me because I smile at him and because I'm Jimmy's friend and maybe because I remind him of his daughter.

Jimmy doesn't know everything about me either. For instance —yesterday's fight with Alyssa—or the fact that Christina Horner jumped me because I stole her Ramones T-shirt out of her gym locker and wouldn't give it back. I don't even know why I did it. She's a junior with a group of mean-looking friends who hang around behind the school, smoking, and anybody else, maybe, would have figured out what would happen, but I guess I felt invisible to her and like the shirt was something I needed.

"Are you crazy?" she said. "Is there something wrong with you?"

I'd had the shirt three months, and this was the first time I'd worn it outside of my bedroom. I thought maybe she'd forgotten about it.

"It's not yours," I kept saying, though we both knew I was lying.

She told me it was her dad's shirt in a way that made me know this meant something to her, but I wouldn't budge, and then she started swinging.

What I was glad about was that she didn't say the most obvious thing, which was that I was dressing up in her clothes, wishing I was her.

"Okay," Jimmy says. He has the money totals written at the bottom of a printout from the cash register and has put the cardboard box of money under the counter again. "I just need to sweep and then I'm out of here. We can take a drive if you want."

By which, I know he means smoke, which is what he does pretty much every day. Me, I've only been high four times total and twice was with him.

The first time I smoked up was in August, with Nicole, back before our fight. We were at a party at the river, sitting on a rock by the campfire, and one of the older girls took apart a cigar and rolled it back up with pot inside. When it got to me, everyone looked to see if I would know what to do, which of course, I didn't really. I breathed in as hard as I could, and kept breathing in even though my throat felt scratched. Then I held my breath. When I let go, I coughed, but in a minute, I was floating and warm and happy, and Nicole was sitting beside me, feeling the same way, and I could tell that we were heading someplace new.

A week later, she told some eighth-grade girls I stuck maxi-pads under my boobs to make them look bigger, and I punched her in the back until someone called a teacher. I got suspended for three days; Nicole got new friends.

While Jimmy's sweeping, Mr. Gorely comes in and wants to know if Jimmy can stay late. He's wearing a pair of khakis and a red flannel shirt with long johns underneath. He isn't smiling, but this is how he always acts. He's thin and has dark hair that he combs over his bald spot and glasses with thick, brown frames. If he didn't frown so much, he wouldn't look mean.

Jimmy looks at me, and I try to signal him by opening my eyes wide that I don't want him to stay.

"I can't," Jimmy says. "Sorry."

We leave my bike at the Citgo station and drive toward town and away from both our houses. His car is his dad's and smells like the cherry air freshener the used car company put through the air-conditioner to wipe out the smoky smell from the last person who owned it. We're listening to the seventies radio station he likes and he's singing along to "Roxanne" in a high-pitched voice and hitting the steering wheel in time to the beat. He's not braking on the hills and my heart keeps jumping. I try to keep my head here, with Jimmy, but I can't stop thinking about Utah and about how my mom keeps saying I need to act right.

"You think you're so tough," she says. "You think you have everything figured out."

When the song ends, the DJ comes on, talking about the twenty minutes of commercial free music that's coming up next.

"We're taking a plane tomorrow," I say. "That should be good at least. I've never flown before."

"Me neither," Jimmy says. "But I took a bus all the way to Florida once with my sister."

Jimmy has known me since the first day of school and our first bus ride home, but that is probably not enough for him to miss me tomorrow. He's probably kissed lots of girls and will probably have another girl to kiss and hang out with when I leave, but for me it's different. He's the first person who kissed me and the first person other than a grown-up to call me pretty.

In town, we pass the BP station and three churches and then the school which is closed up and dark, except for the red exit signs you can see through the windows of the cafeteria. Jimmy drives up the hill past the football field and through the woods at the end of our morning bus route, right before we get to the school. He pulls over onto a sandy patch of dirt beside the guardrail and turns off the engine.

"Check the glove box," he says, and I find a lighter and a box of cigarette papers.

We get out and stand by the edge of a ravine. It's dark and hard to see much, but I know this section of woods. It's above the high school, overlooking the Kiskiminetas River. On the other side of the river is the steel mill in Vandergrift and all of the houses there spread out in little rows. Their steel mill isn't too different from ours except that it's bigger and has a white roof instead of a silver one. From above, the town looks like a play town with a play steel mill and pretend white smoke coming out of the top.

I biked here once with Nicole last summer, looking for blackberries. Leechburg is a small town, and it's hard to find places I haven't been to with her. I still see her, too. We're in classes together, and we go to the same church, and we're even in the same lab group for science, since we picked groups the first day of school, back when we were friends. The hard part is that we still know each other and can tell when the other person will think something is funny or stupid, and so we look at each other every now and then, and I have to remember that we don't talk. I hate it.

Jimmy and I sit down a couple feet from the edge, and the ground is cold, even though it's covered with a layer of leaves. He licks the edge of a cigarette paper and rolls us a joint. He lights it and takes a hit and passes it to me. It hurts my throat, but I take two big hits before passing it back.

"Good shit, right?" he says.

I nod. He puts his arm around me, just loose like, with his hand on my shoulder. It's cold outside, and I let myself lean into him. I've been gone now for almost two hours, and I've ignored the texts from my Mom, which means she's probably called Nicole's house and found out I'm not there. Probably she's in the living room, in her pink nightgown, waiting for me to come home so she can yell.

Tomorrow night, when I'm gone, she can play Scrabble with my sister without having to worry about me sneaking out or punching somebody or stealing cigarettes. According to her, I am going away because she doesn't know what to do with me anymore, but I know her and she's lying. I did everything she said, technically, but I didn't start the fight with Christina, and the other two fights were with my sister and with Nicole, who is like a sister, or was. The knife was something I pulled out at the last minute to be funny, and my sister knew it. Nobody was scared. I'm not going to hurt anybody for real. My mom knows this. She said it. She said, "*I can't take this anymore,*" not, "*You* need help." I'm leaving because she wants me gone.

"You feel it?" he says.

"My head's going to float away."

Jimmy laughs a little and then he puts his hand up my shirt, and then we're lying down, kissing.

I feel weird now—like Jimmy and me could do anything together, and it would be okay. I know it's not real. I know it's the smoke, but my face still feels hot and my lower body feels like someone's pulling a string through my muscles and making them jump. I feel like I did when Jimmy wasn't braking on the hills and my chest was flying, but this is better. This is more like the moment when you give in to a fight. When you don't even care anymore if you win or if your nose is bloody or if someone down the hall's looking at you and laughing. It doesn't matter anymore because you're not there, really, and everything is hazy. You're just pounding someone's back over and over, feeling her muscles give, or you're sinking your teeth into your sister's shoulder.

Even now, though, with my legs tingling, I know I will feel bad tomorrow. I have also heard that you bleed.

"Is this okay?" he says, his hands on my jeans.

"I don't know."

Tomorrow, I'll be out in the desert with girls who are actually tough. I am strong to a point, and prissy girls like Nicole and my sister are scared of me, but if I fight somebody dangerous, I'll just get hurt. My mom thinks she's putting me in an empty space somewhere—a time out, where I can get my act together and she can have some peace—but I know already that something bad will happen.

"Do you think you'll go to Lenape in the fall?" I say.

Lenape is the technical school you can go to in eleventh and twelfth grade if you want to be a hairdresser or mechanic or contractor. I am stalling, and he knows it, but he's letting me. We're on our sides now, facing each other, and his hands are on my ribs, not moving. I can do what I want right now, because in a minute, I will do what Jimmy wants, and he knows it. I could tell him about Nicole or about how scared I am of the group home and scared of myself and scared that everyone will be right not to miss me. I could cry right now, and Jimmy would lie here, waiting.

It is hard, though, to keep my body from rushing toward him with his fingers against my skin. It's simply the next thing that happens—the car flying down the hill, me giving in to a fight, this.

"Probably," Jimmy says. "I could take metal shop at Leechburg, but I want to learn more about cars."

I shift my arm out from under me and run my hand over his sternum, his T-shirt separating our skin.

"You're pretty," he says. "You're really pretty."

I don't want to smile, but I do.

"I'll send you a postcard from the desert," I tell him, but we are against each other, now, tangled, my chin across his shoulder, arms around his waist, and no one's pretending to listen.

A
New
Life

The girl, Hannah, was three and a half weeks old,
two months premature, and small for a newborn. It was November
but warm out that weekend, and the breeze from the open windows filled the house with the smell of wet soil and dead leaves. Nathan was down the hall, asleep in their bedroom, but Rebecca was
right there beside her when it happened, nestled under a faded quilt
on the guest bed, watching her daughter, willing her to sleep. She
turned on the bedside lamp to keep from dozing off in the same bed
with Hannah, which the doctor had told her not to do, but then she
fell asleep anyway. When she woke a few hours later, gray sunlight
filtered through the curtains, and Hannah wasn't breathing.

Rebecca was twenty-five. Since the end of college, she'd worked for an antiques dealer who sold musty wicker furniture out of an old warehouse in Providence, but now she stayed home all day and read self-help books from the library. She'd started with grief but quickly diversified to fashion, home decoration, and easy meals for two. Her favorite books came with photographs of celebrities and clear prohibitions written out in numbered lists. *Low-rise jeans will give pear-shaped women love handles. An entryway, however convenient it may seem to you, is not an appropriate storage space for shoes.* She liked the certainty of right answers and the feeling of building a better life for some future self who might feel like living.

She kept the books hidden in the trunk of her car, away from Nathan, who judged people who wanted to be told what to do. He was a safety engineer for a construction company, seven years older, and an atheist, which she was learning was different than a non-religious person who was pretty sure she didn't believe in God. When she cried, he wrapped his arms around her body, but if she tried to talk about Hannah directly, he accused her of smothering him. One night, he said she was like a drowning swimmer, trying to kill him.

"And this makes you the lifeguard?"

He kicked off the blankets and fumbled around for the reading glasses he would take with him to the couch.

"I'm trying to picture it," she called after him. "I want to know if you think we're both drowning or if it's just me."

At the support group that met twice a month in the beach-themed living room of a Ronald McDonald House, the other mothers of dead infants reassured her this was typical: women fell apart; men got angry.

"He doesn't yell, though," Rebecca said on the phone to her sister Jenny. "He's crabby and a little bit mean. He wants me to shut up and move on."

"Oh, I doubt it," Jenny said. "I'm sure that's not what's happening. Have you heard of the love languages?"

Jenny was divorced with two kids. She had many theories about relationships, most of which came from the Oprah Network that she watched on small monitors at the dental office while she cleaned teeth. "I couldn't tell you his love language, but I'd guess it's not words of affirmation. Does he buy you gifts?"

"Windshield wipers, oil changes."

"Well, that would be acts of service."

Jenny thought Nathan should get credit for putting food on the table and for not pressuring her to have sex with him now that she was back on birth control. Her ex-husband had not been so patient. He'd *seemed* patient, but then he'd had an affair. If Rebecca was up to it, she should go ahead and fuck him. Were there blowjobs?

"Jenny."

"I don't like the thought of you losing him. On top of everything else, I don't want to think about you going through this alone."

Rebecca told her sister to mind her own business, but then she couldn't stop wondering if Nathan would leave. She didn't think so, but then again, she didn't *not* think so. He worked long hours, stayed up late drinking whiskey and watching *Law & Order*. He did what he could to not be home.

In February, Rebecca initiated sex and then locked herself in the bathroom, crying. Through the filmed windowpane above the bathtub, her neighbors' house lights smeared across the darkness. She sat on the linoleum floor and stared at the linty fur along the heater grate, blowing in small curtains that looked as if they would shake loose but didn't.

In May, Nathan pulled a thick manila envelope from his briefcase and set it on the glass coffee table, frayed on its edges and missing a piece of the outer flap. Divorce papers? She imagined him carrying the envelope around for months, waiting for a respectable amount of time to pass before he was allowed to flee.

"Go ahead," she said. "Tell me."

Nathan was wearing a striped Oxford shirt, still tucked into his dress pants but wrinkled, and his face had the wilted look of the end of a long workweek. "It's a job promotion," he said. "It's a shit ton of money, but it's in Abu Dhabi."

She turned toward him. She had heard of Abu Dhabi but was pretty sure she couldn't find it on a map. "You'd move there?"

"No," he said. "We would. The two of us."

In Abu Dhabi, they lived in a large sandstone villa on a man-made island by the airport with vaulted ceilings and marble floors, modern furniture rented from a company catalogue. The house was twice the size of their house in Rhode Island, a century newer, filled with chrome appliances and walk-in closets that smelled like cedar, but their subdivision was surrounded by empty lots of gray sand snarled with bulldozers and machines. All night heavy trucks groaned past on the highway, and workers hammered through the dark under floodlit cranes. It was July and staggeringly hot. Thick air, no breeze, a bright constant sun angled low in the sky.

Nathan worked six days a week and played soccer in the evenings, coming home at eight o'clock on early nights, nine or ten o'clock if they went out for drinks, but it no longer felt like he was avoiding her so much as learning to be happy. He liked Abu Dhabi. He saw the money he could earn, the gadgets he could buy, the international community of businessmen waiting to befriend him, and Rebecca saw a country of strangers, temporarily living beside each other. Everyone seemed lonely to her and on edge, and whenever she went anywhere by herself, she was aware that people were staring. The Emirati women stared with a kind of recognition, the Emirati men stared with mild curiosity, and the hordes of construction workers, shipped in from India and Pakistan, stared at her with an unblinking intensity that made her look away.

"It's lust," Nathan said. "They think you look like a movie star."

"It's not lust."

She was standing at the shimmering granite countertop, slicing lunch-sized chunks of lasagna into Tupperware containers, and he was moving back and forth behind her, clearing the table.

"Do they bother you?" he said, angry on her behalf. "If they bother you, you can call the police."

"They don't bother me," she said. "They stare. It's tiring."

One day, she took a taxi to a glittering high-ceilinged mall by the marina, where gleaming walkways circled a blue-floored fountain and giant palm trees twinkled with tiny lights. By the front entrance, two men in green construction jumpsuits gaped at a storefront advertisement of a British model in her underwear and then looked at Rebecca as if she were trespassing. She walked past coffee shops of young Emirati men in long white robes, a sea of perfume spritzers, and barely-attended children running in circles. She took an escalator down to a giant fluorescent-lit grocery in the basement and bought a bottle of water and an almond croissant. In the checkout line, a toffee-haired toddler looked up at her from behind his mother's skirts and pointed, his tiny fist squeezing open and closed.

Most days, she stayed home, cooking and cleaning. She watched dubbed American television shows, listened to a British pop radio station, wrote upbeat e-mails to Jenny and her parents about the lush hotels and skyscrapers, and tried not to think about the loneliness that tugged at her chest like an anchor. Her old life was far away, but her grief felt closer, somehow, and stronger. Alone all day, estranged from everything she knew, her inner life magnified, and all of the thoughts she had tried to bury swam to the surface like a simmering pot of stock dislodging fat from bone. What she didn't want to know came in two lists. The good list— the harder, longer list about Hannah's childhood, the foods she would have liked, the subjects she would have preferred in school, whether her blonde hair and blue eyes would have darkened, and then, the bad list. For instance, was it Rebecca's fault? She dreamed of crushing Hannah's skull in her sleep, suffocating her with blankets, covering her mouth with the palm of her hand.

In the daytime, she drifted in her own private fog, but no one, not even Nathan, seemed to notice. One Saturday in August, they went out with Nathan's coworkers to Trader Vic's, a low-lit French-Polynesian chain restaurant inside a hotel by the beach. A Colombian band was playing salsa onstage, and they sat outside at a table on the grass by the pool where it was quieter—the men, along with one female architect, on one side of the table, and Rebecca on the other side with the wives. The men ordered beer and talked about work, and the women ordered fruity drinks that came with toothpick umbrellas and complimented each other on the cocktail dresses they were all wearing. Rebecca, who had worn linen pants and a loose tunic, explained that before she'd left the United States, she'd purchased clothing to match a diagram she'd found online of "acceptable outfits" for visitors to the Grand Mosque.

"I was proud of myself," she said. "I really thought these ugly clothes would help me fit in."

The wives stared at her with a quiet, cliquish disdain, and

the female architect, a dark-haired cherub-faced woman from the Netherlands, gave her a quick smile before abruptly looking away.

"You're overthinking it there," said a short plump blonde whose freckled arms squeezed against the armholes of her dress. "It's not Afghanistan."

A redheaded Australian screwed up her face. "Let them stare at me," she said. "They can get over it. It's not like I'm walking around with my tits out."

She nodded, but it was too late. Rebecca and these women did not belong to the same tribe. Like her, they were housewives with no work visas or job prospects, no real place in this country, but unlike her, this did not depress them.

The next week, Rebecca signed up for an Arabic class that met three times a week in a windowless classroom at a Muslim community center. The teacher, Abdullah, was a disheveled, potbellied man from Jordan who brought a thermos of sticky-sweet tea for them each class and told elaborate jokes about marriage that no one got. "It's funny," he would say. "You must believe me. My bad English ruins the joke."

Often, though, he did make Rebecca laugh simply because he was happy and good-natured and his limited English warped his everyday sentences into strange declarations. One day, when they were learning the names of animals, he hadn't known how to explain the difference between domesticated animals and ones that were wild.

"Pet?" someone had guessed. "Livestock?"

"No!" he said. "The one that eats the peoples."

Nathan didn't understand the practical purpose of learning Arabic in a country where pretty much everyone spoke English, but she could tell he liked the stories she told him about Abdullah and appreciated the effort she was making to like it here. At night, lying beside each other in the pitch dark, the streetlights blocked out by the heavy wall-to-wall drapes, the faint swoosh of traffic in the distance, she pressed her face against the musky crook of his neck, and he listened to her without the usual undercurrent of defensiveness. He laughed at her jokes, heard her complaints, agreed with whatever she told him, though she often had the feeling that he wasn't really listening. Coiled against him, her breathing synced with the rise and fall of his chest, a frightened lonely feeling came over her like a distant warning siren. Did he love her? Had he ever loved her? If he gave himself permission to leave a woman whose child had died, how long would it take him to go?

In October, Nathan had a long weekend for a Muslim holiday Abdullah called "Little Eid," and he surprised her by suggesting a trip to Muscat. They left in a rented car just before sunrise. Against the early light, the office buildings and construction sites sat dark and idle. Beyond the city, waves of red sand followed the highway for long empty miles.

At the UAE exit checkpoint, the young bearded man behind the Plexiglas looked back and forth between them and their passports for what seemed like a very long time and asked them a question in English about Nathan's work visa that they couldn't understand. He left the window, and an older man replaced him. This man had alert dark eyes, a faint line of hair between his eyebrows, and something kind and curious in his expression that reminded her of Abdullah.

She leaned past Nathan and said hello to him in Arabic and wished him a happy Eid. The questions this time were standard ones—the length of the visit and their final destination—but for some reason, Rebecca found herself saying how surprised she was that her husband was taking a vacation.

"He's a stubborn husband," she said. "His love is work. Husbands never love family so much as wives."

She smiled to let the man know that she was making a joke, but he didn't react. She didn't know enough Arabic to explain.

Nathan gave her a quizzical look, and then, miraculously, the guard was laughing.

"The wife is in charge," he told Nathan in English, tilting his head toward him and smiling with a kind of happy, reassured exasperation as if to say, *Women, what can you do?*

Past the border, coppery mountains sprang up on either side of the road, and drift sand billowed across the highway. When Rebecca tried the radio, only Islamic chanting and static crackled through the channels. There was a sense of desolation that made her mind wander, and it took a minute to realize that Nathan had asked her a question.

"What did you say to him?"

She unfolded the map of Oman they picked up at the border, a thick detailed map that anticipated lots of English-speaking tourists. Supposedly, their current location was one of the more populated areas, but the landscape looked deserted.

"Nothing. I was just talking."

"Tell me."

She opened the glove box and pretended to examine the owner's manual.

"What did you say to him?" he repeated.

"I said you don't like spending time with me."

"No you didn't."

"No," she said. "But it's what I meant to say. My Arabic sucks."

She felt the slow reeling of a fight building. She knew she should apologize but that she wouldn't. Nathan's breathing quickened, settled, then quickened again.

"I can't be the only one of us who's ever nice," he said, finally. "I can't always be the one who's trying. Are you listening?"

"Yes," Rebecca said, evenly, though the conversation felt far away. "You are trying, and I am not trying, and this is unfair to you."

They drove southeast through the mountains and into the sun, past date farms, grazing goats, honeycombed limestone forts, and signs warning that rocks might fall. The rocks glinted pink and gold in the sun, and grey-blue shadows floated between the hillsides of shaded homes bordered by irrigation ditches.

She slipped the owner's manual back into the glove box and latched the door.

"I don't know why you haven't left me, but I'm not crazy," she said. "I can tell the difference between you wanting to be with me and you not leaving."

"I love you," he said, calmly. "I want to love you."

"You want to love me?"

They stopped talking. When the hillsides softened, and the narrow roads grew thick with traffic and construction barriers,

Nathan stopped for gas and then moved the car to the edge of the parking lot. They leaned against opposite corners of the Toyota's dusty bumper and ate the egg salad sandwiches Rebecca had made.

He pressed his thumbs against the muscles between shoulder and neck, loosening the tension of driving, and she put her hand against his.

"Here." She rubbed her fingers against his muscles and tried not to acknowledge the stares of the gas station attendants. "I'm sorry."

She looked at her tennis shoes, a few months old but already discolored by light brown dust, and then Nathan, who was squinting at her face, shading his eyes with one hand, balancing the squashed pieces of his sandwich with the other. She couldn't read his expression.

"I'm sorry," she said again. "I'm—"

"I slept with someone."

Rebecca could feel him watching her, but she made herself look forward at the giant wave-shaped awning looming over a sea of gray brick. She half-listened to him telling her that he was sorry, that it was over now, that he hadn't meant to tell her like this. She waited for her anger to kick in, but she felt only a low thrum of queasiness and regret, the murky underwater feeling that something shameful about her had been revealed.

He wanted to know if they should go home.

"To Abu Dhabi?"

"We can turn around," he said. "We can drive back right now if you want."

"We bought a tent," she said. "We're here."

In Muscat, they parked their car in the old quarter and walked along a sidewalk by the sea, where commercial ships rocked against a stone seawall. Rebecca stared at hillsides of square uniformly white houses and Nathan watched her with the guilty patience of someone who had resigned himself to a long penance. She had thought he meant he'd slept with someone in Rhode Island, but it was the Dutch architect whose face she now remembered as patronizing and matronly. She lived in Kuwait, and they had seen each other only a handful of times. Mostly, it had been e-mails, he said, and mostly, the e-mails had been about Rebecca. He'd tried to complain about his marriage, but the woman, who had lost her mother in a car accident at age twelve, had always taken Rebecca's side.

"That's supposed to make me feel better?" Rebecca had screamed at him.

The architect had told him to listen without justifying himself or fixing anything, which he seemed to think was a revelation and which Rebecca understood was responsible for his dopey meditative silences, listening as if she were a radio lulling him to sleep.

When it was midafternoon, they got back into the car and drove farther south, past rocky cliffs slung over the sea, waves crashing below them, and stopped the car on the edge of a large expanse of empty white sand. They pitched the tent and walked toward the ocean to watch the sunset. They took off their shoes, walked in the foam of waves, and watched a group of boys in the distance kicking a soccer ball. In comparison to Abu Dhabi's high-rise beach resorts, the beach felt unspoiled but lonesome.

Nathan reached for her hand, and a flare of desire lit through her body. How had this happened? He'd taken her across the world to abandon her, and now she wanted him.

"I hate you," she'd said again and again in the car, though the more she said it, the more the feeling diminished. She did hate him, a little, but it was a small feeling beside the ache she felt now, in spite of herself, to be loved.

The sun hung above the faint line of the mountains, a pale circle in a dusty pink and yellow sky, and the trees along the shore became dark, prickling shadows. In the distance, the call to prayer sounded, and the boys with the soccer ball paused their game and knelt together on the sand. Rebecca stopped walking and stood still, as if she, too, were observing the ritual. She knew she needed to think.

They were putting on their shoes when one of the soccer players called out to them and then came over, holding the hand of a toddler. *"Arabie?"*

Rebecca nodded and said "little" in Arabic.

The man spoke rapidly, but she understood enough to know he was inviting them to join a celebration. Without asking Nathan, she agreed. They walked through a brick courtyard lined with bougainvillea, and the man explained that because children were permitted to go to both the men's and women's parties, his son would take Rebecca to his wife. It occurred to her that Nathan didn't know any Arabic, but the thought of him silenced and struggling lifted her spirits.

She followed the boy to a large room of low, gold-threaded couches, where dozens of women in ball gowns were eating food and watching a large flat-screen television playing music videos in Arabic. Except for the foreign women serving the food, no one's head was covered, and everyone's hair was fixed in elaborate curls and twists. The boy led her to a pretty young woman in a purple rhinestone-studded dress, and Rebecca wondered what kind of person she must look like barging in this way in hiking pants and a long-sleeved T-shirt.

The woman shook her hand and gave her a look of friendly but uncertain welcome. "Thank you," Rebecca said in Arabic. She gestured to the room and said *"Mash'Allah,"* the word to say in praise of someone while protecting them from jealousy, the verbal equivalent of an evil eye.

Rebecca washed her hands, followed the woman toward a banquet table piled high with lamb and salads, pastries, dates, rice, and then to a circle of young women spread out on the floor. She began to squat down, but the woman pointed to a wooden chair beside a heavy old woman in a wheelchair with a pouch of clear liquid dripping into a vein. She shook the old woman's bony hand and fought the urge to recoil. She thought of how Abdullah had bragged that his country did not have homeless shelters or nursing homes because, in his country, a family did not let you get discarded.

Almost as soon as she sat down, a wave of fatigue washed over her. Nathan—thinking about Nathan—had worn her out. He didn't seem as if he'd wanted to hurt her. In fact, he sounded almost proud of himself. Not proud of the affair but of the way it had changed him. He'd become a better man, a better more empathetic listener, and, preposterously, he wanted Rebecca to tell him he had done a good job.

On the other side of her chair, a group of young women flipped through a photograph album and giggled with nervous excitement. When one of the girls noticed Rebecca watching them, she asked about Rebecca's wedding ring and husband, and Rebecca passed around a picture of Nathan saved on her phone. She repeated phrases she had practiced many times in her Arabic classes—"We are from America. We live in Abu Dhabi. My husband is Nathan. He works as an engineer."—but she knew she was describing a life that no longer belonged to her.

She felt a hand on her shoulder and turned to see the host sitting beside the woman in the wheelchair—her mother? her grandmother?—and leaning toward Rebecca. "Engagement book," she said in careful English. "For wedding."

The two women seemed to want to talk about their traditions, and so she asked about their own marriages and if they had engagement pictures.

"Yes," the young woman said tentatively. "Maybe."

Rebecca pointed to the engagement book and then to the old woman. "You have?"

The old woman laughed, shook her head, and then the younger woman explained that there were no cameras to document a wedding so long ago, and Rebecca realized that the old woman had grown up before the oil boom. She had a vague awareness that she should pay attention, that this was a woman who had crossed over from an older, simpler time, but she knew only the words to ask about what she least wanted to know—family.

"Do you have children?"

The woman said yes, eight children. The host was child number seven. Rebecca stared into the woman's face, half expecting her to confess that she had lost other children in childbirth, but she didn't. When the woman asked about Rebecca's family, she hesitated and then shook her head. It was cruel and complicated to tell the truth, but lying about Hannah made her hate herself.

"Someday," the younger woman said in Arabic. "*Insha'Allah.*"

The women's faces told her that this was sad news, but she couldn't tell if they saw her pain or if this was simply how they would look at any childless woman.

"*Haram,*" said the older woman, squeezing Rebecca's hand. The word made her startle the way it often did, though in this context, she knew it did not mean "forbidden" but something like "what a shame" or "I'm sorry," one of those everyday phrases that sounded prophetic but wasn't.

When she saw Nathan across the courtyard, he was in the midst of a dynamic conversation with a young man in glasses, their bodies illuminated by the glow of the lanterns. They were talking fast and laughing, and it took Rebecca a moment to realize that they were speaking English. Of course. The men lived in a wider orbit—were likelier to have been educated abroad, likelier to encounter foreigners at work. Why did Rebecca assume anything else? Men went through life like this—mobile, unselfconscious, unafraid. The world did not expect them to adapt to other people or justify their presence, and this made them strong, but also, stupid. They were not taught to test their visions of themselves against the judgments of strangers, and this meant they could reach adulthood without ever having had to wonder who they were. She had thought that Nathan hid his emotions because he was brave or stingy or else because he simply did not care. It had not occurred to her to see him as helpless.

She steadied herself against the house and made her lungs keep breathing. Beyond the latticed stone walls, stars scattered across the black sky, and the ocean crashed against the shore. Nathan lifted his hand to wave and looked at her with an expression of certainty and determination. A man who had been tasked with a great responsibility and believed himself capable of answering. He was ready to stay with her now, ready to make it work. She imagined what advice she would get from Jenny, the support group, the self-help books from the library, but she knew, somehow, that she wouldn't tell anyone. What had happened between them was theirs—a secret thing between them.

On the morning, when Hannah had already died but the EMTs had not yet come to look at her body, she had sat on the edge of their king-sized bed with Hannah in her arms, waiting for Nathan to open his eyes. He was lying with a pillow held over his head, restless, trying to fall back asleep. She had woken him up screaming, but then, somehow, his fatigue had won out. Eventually, she would add this moment to the tally of things she held against him, but in the long calm of the gray light, an unseasonably warm November breeze, she had understood. She had wanted him to keep sleeping. She had hoped he would never have to know.

The
House
Always
Wins

_____

The third time they slept together, they woke to the sound of sirens. They were at Ethan's apartment, one of six units in a skinny modern building on the grounds of the Gibson Day School, where he had recently taken a job as a "visiting poet," which had turned out to mean "low-paid teacher." Marcie was standing in front of his panoramic bedroom window, wearing one of his white undershirts and a pair of sporty cotton briefs, and he was watching the flex of her small butt as she peered through the glass.

She was twenty-eight, a year older than Ethan, a chemistry teacher at Gibson, and a lesbian. They'd bonded over their love of whiskey and their heartache over having recently been dumped by women who were too good for them, and then, to his amazement, they'd had sex. Initially, he'd felt proud of himself for seducing a lesbian, but she told him not to take it personally, that she preferred to have casual sex with straight men who were plentiful and unlikely to get attached.

"So, you're bi?" he'd said. "That's cool."

"Not bi," she said. "*Gay.*"

"Okay," he said and pretended, as he did with many things these days, that this made sense to him.

He turned on the lamp beside his bed and put on his glasses.

"It could be another Forever Home fire," Marcie was saying now. "Aren't you curious?"

He shrugged. His head pounded from the bottle of WhistlePig they'd polished off the night before, and Marcie was topless, looking for her bra. Her breasts were full and round with small erect nipples whose muted pink reminded him of the inside of a conk shell, and though just a few hours ago, he'd cupped her breasts in his hands while fucking her from behind, he understood that ogling her now, the morning after, was a transgression.

"You okay?" she said. "You look ill."

He nodded without making eye contact. "I'll start the coffee."

They followed the smoke past the manicured lawns and brick buildings of Gibson to a sprawl of mansions along the water. It was October, chilly, and a cloud-streaked sky stretched above them, dotted with a handful of fat bright stars. They'd brought brown sugar Pop-Tarts along with their mugs of coffee, and Ethan was thinking about how thirsty he was when they saw the police barricade, the mass of people in their pajama pants and slippers, and then the ostentatious pink mansion in the distance, burning. A cloud of orange flames licked through the middle of the main roof and lit up the turrets and their party-hat shaped roofs like eerie shadow puppets. In front of the house, the branches of naked oaks reached up like dark claws. The air smelled like burning chemicals. The house was set back from the road at the end of its own long private driveway, and it looked almost moderately sized until you realized that the fluorescent yellow dots scattering around its perimeter were fire fighters.

"Oh my God," Ethan said, but Marcie was watching the fire tear through the house, not listening.

He'd heard about the Forever Home Project on the national news like everybody else, but now that he was here in St. Anne's, it was all people talked about. The technology had been developed to protect the multimillion dollar homes along the Chesapeake Bay from the effects of climate change and came in two varieties—the factory model that started at a little under five million and the cheaper upgraded home package that added stainless steel enhancements to a traditional home and coated its exterior and interior surfaces with a halogenated polymer that was both flood-resistant and self-extinguishing. A Forever Home could be submerged in water for seventy-two hours without suffering significant damage. It could withstand 150-mile-an-hour winds. And most spectacularly, if a Forever Home caught fire, it would burn until it reached sixty percent heat saturation, and then it would automatically self-extinguish and reconstitute.

The people in Saint Anne's were proud of the Forever Homes, but recently, underneath the pride, lay a palpable sense of dread. In the past three months, seven Forever Homes had caught fire, and no one could satisfactorily explain why. There were rumors that the SnapBack polymer degraded over time, releasing unstable gases that were susceptible to combustion, but the Forever Home Company denied that this was true. They encouraged homeowners to take "regular safeguards" and cautioned against the false sense of security that might result from living in a home with such "unprecedented safety features."

Not far from Marcie and Ethan, a woman with springy white hair was staring up at the fire and whispering to her friend. "It's not normal," she was saying. "It looks like an oil spill caught fire."

The woman was wearing a men's denim jean jacket and red flannel pajama pants pushed into the shafts of her rubber-soled work boots, and it occurred to Ethan, as it often did lately, that these women might be lesbians. He didn't trust himself to know the difference. With Marcie, even after she'd pointed out the signs—her short nails, her industrial toolbox—he hadn't been able to see her as anyone other than a girl who drove him crazy. She was pretty in a careless haphazard way, and sex with her was easily the best he'd had, which he found to be both electrifying and unsettling. Just being around her made him feel poisoned.

They waited while the sun rose above the water and the house continued to burn. The flames rolled across the roof and then radiated down along the siding. Black smoke rose from the house, but the frame stayed intact. The firefighters sprayed the yard and the trees with water, and an ambulance waited in the driveway with its back doors open.

"Do you think anybody's in there?" Ethan said.

Marcie nodded toward a young couple with two small children huddled together on the other side of the police barricade, and then she was grabbing his elbow and pointing at the house.

It happened in stages. The clouds of fire shrank back; the black smoke began to thin; the flames slid back into the house like a gas burner slowly swallowing its ring of heat. For a long moment, the edges of the roof glittered with red-orange embers that pulsed bright and dark, as if the house were breathing. And then this too was gone, and they could see the blackened frame slowly regaining its color and substance until it was solid again and shimmering with the gloss of new paint. A wave of relief shivered through the crowd, and all around him, people were cheering and laughing. The only signs of the fire were the veil of steam that hung over the yard and the smell of sulphurous smoke.

Ethan had moved from Lincoln, Nebraska, five months ago, and even before the fires had started, he'd thought St. Anne's was a confounding place. Often, particularly at Gibson, he had the sense that people were speaking in a code that everybody but him understood. In the Midwest, people said things indirectly—avoided what wasn't their business, said "maybe" when they really meant "no"—but here, it was more like people said what they wished was true and then waited to see if it would happen.

Today, for instance, nearly a week after the most recent house fire, the theme of their Friday school-wide assembly was "Forever Homes: Advantages and Responsibilities." The message of the whole assembly was that although the Forever Homes seemed more dangerous than traditional homes, they were actually safer. There had been a slide show, a speech from someone at the development company, and now Kyla Henderson and Dylan Mack, two sophomore girls who were both in his introductory poetry class were on stage, performing a skit. Kyla, a sweet giggly kid who wrote vague sentimental poetry about the ocean, was taking the lead, and her friend, Dylan, was shuffling behind her. Dylan was a slightly better writer than Kyla but sullen and hard to like. She'd gotten a B+ for the first quarter and now refused to make eye contact in their weekly meetings. Instead, she argued with him about her poems.

"I couldn't put in more concrete details because *you* won't let us go over 100 lines." Or, "I *did* use a lot of images. Do you want me to show you?"

Whenever he saw Dylan, he wanted to slap her and explain how lucky she was to go to a high school that offered poetry classes and employed a "teaching artist" who was compelled to meet one-on-one with students every single goddamn week.

The premise of the skit was that Kyla and Dylan had put cookies in the oven and couldn't decide if it was okay to run to the store.

"I know we're not supposed to leave the oven on when we're not home," said Kyla. "But what's the point of living in a Forever Home if we're always thinking about house fires?"

"So true," said Dylan.

The girls ambled around the stage, miming the motions of driving and grocery shopping. Then, they came back to the edge of the stage where they'd started and covered their mouths in exaggerated shock.

"It looks like our house *did* burn down," said Dylan. "But it snapped back. No harm, right?"

"Right," said Kyla. "My parents won't even notice."

At this point, the back curtain opened, revealing a shaggy-haired junior lacrosse player, lying on his back, wriggling. The audience cheered.

"Oh my God!" said Kyla. "Fluffy."

"Is Fluffy . . . dead?"

Kyla pretended to cry while Dylan hugged her, and then both girls turned back to the audience and said in unison, "The house snaps back, but people and pets won't."

Ethan couldn't make sense of the agenda behind the assembly. It felt like propaganda, but he couldn't figure out why Gibson cared so much about the Forever Home Company.

"Money. What else?" This was Jim Keppler, the anxious, perpetually sweaty American literature teacher who lived in the apartment above Ethan. They were sitting on Keppler's balcony, high above the bright green lacrosse fields, drinking gin and tonics. Keppler had graduated from an elite New England boarding school two decades ago and seemed hopeful that Gibson would someday become a good enough school to re-create this time in his life. Conversations with him were always tedious and often competitive, but because Ethan was lonely and because Keppler was the one who'd hired him, he spent a fair amount of time voluntarily listening to him.

"It's not just their campus properties," Keppler explained. "Half the parents have stock in that company, and the parents are the ones who fund our school."

"But are they safe?"

The balcony walls were made from thin metal cables, and in the bright afternoon sun, they almost disappeared.

"Oh no, these things are fucking time bombs," Keppler said. "We're getting out at the end of the year. They're threatening to cut my salary, but fuck it. Beth's pregnant."

"Is that true?" he asked Marcie that Saturday afternoon. "Should I be moving?"

She began to talk about explosive limits and ignition sources, and then, when it became obvious that he didn't understand science very well, she said, "Short answer, probably."

This unnerved him. He certainly didn't want to live in an exploding apartment, but even if he managed to get out of his lease, he wasn't sure where he would go. St. Anne's was in the third wealthiest county in the nation, and the Gibson teaching salaries were livable only because they came with housing and lunches in the cafeteria. Almost all of the teachers lived on campus.

Marcie was an exception. She'd moved to Maryland a year and a half ago with her then girlfriend, Kate, who was a medical resident at Johns Hopkins, and they'd bought a rundown row house in Baltimore, an hour's drive from Gibson. The neighborhood was a mix of African American families who'd lived in these houses for generations and white twenty-somethings who wore thrift store

T-shirts and put anarchist bumper stickers on their cars. Marcie's house was gray formstone with two levels of small rooms bisected by a staircase that wound through the center of the house. The floors were covered by plastic drop cloths and plaster dust, and the walls smelled like old smoke.

That afternoon, he was helping her sand down the unevenly spackled walls in the living room and listening to her obsess over the new girlfriend she'd seen Kate holding hands with at the farmers' market. He was also trying to figure out if he had a crush on her. He liked her competence with power drills, her compact muscles, the unselfconsciousness with which she sang along off-key to Bob Seger. Was this just lust? His last girlfriend, Lindsay, a woman he'd dated for five years and assumed he would marry, had often told him what a nice guy he was, and because she had rarely meant this as a compliment, he'd assumed it was true. Lately, though, he wondered if he was really just an asshole in waiting, a guy who wanted to disrespect women but hadn't yet found the courage.

"I think you have to put it out of your mind," he said finally. "That's what I did with Lindsay. If you let yourself keep thinking about it, you're always going to care."

Marcie changed the subject, but he could tell she wanted to say more about Kate.

They worked until they were slick with sweat and then took separate showers, and Marcie ordered a pizza. They stayed up late drinking and playing cards, and then, when she was finally buzzed enough to let him touch her, he followed her upstairs to her bedroom, where she lay him down on her bed and began to peel off her clothes. Underneath her sweatshirt and jeans, she was wearing a see-through black lace bra and matching underwear.

She straddled him and rubbed the crotch of her underwear against him, and then before he knew it, she was pressing her naked body against his and whispering into his ear that she wanted him to fuck her hard. The desire seemed real, violent, ravenous, and he had to remind himself not to take any of this too seriously. He rolled her over onto her back and watched her breath quicken while he thrust inside her. Her eyes were closed and her mouth was open.

"Oh God," she kept saying. "Oh *God*."

Sex with Marcie was rougher than it had been with any of the other women he'd slept with and his only experience having sex with a woman who could have an orgasm simply from vaginal penetration. He pounded against her, and she lifted her legs to take more. He grabbed her hair, and she told him to slap her. It was doing something weird to his mind.

In his life so far, there had been two long-term girlfriends and a few more casual affairs with women he sort of knew, and until this point in his life, sex had always been a compromise. He had trained himself to be more gentle and patient than he wanted, and in return, most of the girls he slept with wanted to do it again. With Marcie though, his patience bored her. She wanted sex to be brutal, athletic. He found himself imagining violence—forcing her, hurting her, calling her names.

"Don't stop," Marcie was saying now. "Oh God. Like that."

They were sitting on her bed, her legs wrapped around his hips, slamming against him. Her eyes were shut tight, and she was screaming, the way she always did right when she got close. He liked this part and the part after, when her eyes would open, and she would look at him like she was waking up from a dream. Every time his breath would catch, thinking that she would realize the mistake she'd made, but she would just grin at him and pull him close, guiding him to the end.

After, they ate ice-cream sandwiches at a card table in Marcie's kitchen, and then she was talking about Kate's girlfriend again, and he felt his attachment to her draining away. He was annoyed by the way she sat with her legs wide open, the way she ate as if she were starving and alone. It felt as if she was going out of her way to act like a lesbian.

"She looks like she's about twelve," she said. "Did I show you her picture?"

She hadn't, but he nodded. She was rotating her ice-cream sandwich, methodically lapping at the melting vanilla. He felt a quick stab of disgust for her, but it was accompanied by a wave of desire. He imagined pressing himself against her mouth and pulling her hair, calling her a whore. She'd never given him a blowjob before, and it made him sad, almost angry, to know that she probably never would.

In November, there were two more Forever Home fires, one of which resulted in the asphyxiation of a retired couple people especially liked, and a small group of community members began to organize. The Forever Home warranties were good for just two years, and insurance rates were skyrocketing. People were scared to go to sleep at night but felt they had invested too much to walk away.

Keppler, who was still fighting with Gibson over his contract, went to all of the meetings and kept trying to get Ethan involved. He was angry with the Forever Home Company for misleading consumers and angry with the state government for relaxing building codes to accommodate for the homes' combustible, insufficiently tested chemicals, and he was angry with Gibson for forming a partnership with the Forever Home Company that was endangering the lives of its teachers.

"I don't get how people aren't rioting," he kept saying. "We're living in a science experiment that's going to explode."

"People care," Ethan said, meaning, "*I* care," but he still didn't go to the meetings. The company seemed too powerful to be held responsible, and he was afraid that knowing more about his apartment would make him panic. The only solution he could see was to wait it out and then find a new job at the end of the school year.

That month, all of the teachers in their building agreed to follow a set of restrictive guidelines—no candles, no space heaters, no use of the oven or stove—and when they all got together at Keppler's apartment for Thanksgiving dinner, the meal was depressing. Rubbery casseroles and canned vegetables, a dry cooked-in-the-microwave apple pie. The turkey, which had been baked in Marcie's house in Baltimore was okay but cold. After dinner, they played charades and drank several bottles of wine, and by the time Ethan and Marcie stumbled down to his apartment, he was in a bad mood and angry with Marcie, who had told him earlier in the week that she'd slept with Kate.

"Why do you sleep with me?" he said. "I mean, like this? Why do you stay over?"

She had stripped down to her T-shirt and underwear and was lying beside him, under the covers. Although they weren't touching, he could feel the heat radiating from her bare legs.

"You lie around in your underwear. You talk about your sex life like I'm your pal. You—it's confusing."

"Okay," she said slowly, and flipped on a lamp. "Maybe we should stop." She had propped herself up on her elbow and was watching him with a cautiousness that made him feel vulnerable and immature.

They lay there for a moment, not talking, and then she smiled shyly. "It's like my superpower," she said. "I can have great sex with a guy and have no emotions."

Hearing her talk this way sent a sudden jolt to his genitals.

"You think we have great sex?"

"You don't?"

He straddled her and tugged at her pants. He expected her to push him away and when she didn't, he grabbed a condom from his bedside table, pinned her arms above her head, and then he shoved into her before she was probably ready. He watched her face for signs that he was hurting her, but she looked about the same as always. The next morning, she had faint thumb-shaped bruises on her wrists, but when he apologized, she told him to shut up about it, and then they had sex again.

They had nearly three weeks off for Christmas break, and he spent the entire time at his parents' house in Hebron, Nebraska, a small town of rolling farmland in the southeastern region of the state, trying to forget about Marcie and make a plan for the end of the school year. He ate three hot meals a day, went to bed early, slept late. His parents' house was dark, quiet, surrounded on all sides by fallow fields and crop cover, and almost immediately, he felt his body relaxing. At Christmas dinner, his sister and her husband who were visiting from Omaha listened to his stories about Gibson and about the Forever Homes and said that he should move back to Nebraska and teach high school full time.

"I don't see the big problem," his mom said. "You can write poems in the summer."

"I'd need a teaching certificate," he said. "And maybe a lobotomy."

Later, outside in the cold, walking the dogs, nearly freezing their asses off, his sister said that the job prospects for lawyers were nearly as bad as they were for poets and that the key to being happy was lowering your standards. "Look at me," she said. "I work for a personal injury firm that advertises on late night television. My boss calls himself 'The Force.' It's basically a joke, except it's not that bad."

He smiled.

"Seriously," she said. "I pay my bills, and I have Rick. It's better than it sounds."

The farms were sheared bare for the winter, flat acres of nubbly wheat and cornstalks as far as the eye could see. Looking at them gave him an expansive feeling, a sense that he had more time in his life than he'd thought.

"I'm not saying give up or anything, but I don't know," she said. "You're not obligated to be a starving artist forever."

When the dogs finally finished, and they were headed back inside, Ethan felt disappointed. He had the urge to unburden himself. He wanted to say something about Marcie but what? That she consumed him? That the lust he felt for her was ugly? That maybe, underneath it all, he was a bad person?

"I'm sleeping with a lesbian," was what he ended up saying, and his sister just laughed.

When his sister went home, he still had another two weeks left, which he mostly spent reading paperback novels from the public library and eating grilled cheese sandwiches. On his last night, he went to a bar with a friend and ran into his high school girlfriend, Joanie, who had two kids who she told him several times were spending the night with her ex-husband. She was chubbier than she had been in high school, prettier than he'd remembered, and more at ease. She laughed often and with her whole body. After a pitcher of beers and two games of darts, she took him home to a small house that was covered with plastic toys and smelled like meatloaf, and then they had sex. It was nice, friendly. It felt like getting a massage.

Afterwards, she put on long johns and a pair of wool knee socks and went to sleep, and Ethan lay awake in the pitch black, thinking about Marcie and her body. He missed her but wished he didn't.

In the morning, Joanie made him baked oatmeal and asked him to help her chop a fallen tree branch into logs. It felt like he had been transported into a different decade, and then, just like that, he was gone.

He had a midday flight, and his cousin Andrew's kid, Caleb, drove him the hour and a half to the Lincoln airport. He was a senior in high school, a smart talkative kid who was hoping to go to the University of Nebraska in the fall to study engineering. His fallback, and the only other school he was applying to, was the satellite campus in Omaha.

"You know, either way," he said. "They're both probably good."

It was easy to imagine Caleb's future as a happy one—four years of college followed by a wife and kids, a nice house in the Midwestern suburbs—but Ethan's acceptance of his lot in life made Ethan angry. At Gibson, the students had SAT prep classes and a team of guidance counselors who edited their college essays. They had alumni connections, Ivy League recruitments for sailing and other sports that only rich people could afford to play. Their fallback schools were places like Tufts and Middlebury, and having to go to these schools made the students cry.

On the plane ride home, he tried to imagine what it would be like to be Joanie's boyfriend again and decided he should probably stop talking to Marcie and join a dating site. But when the plane landed, he saw a missed call from her, and his resolve weakened. He only made it as far as the park-n-ride where he'd left his car before he called her back.

When she answered the phone, she was crying.

"What is it?" he said, deflated. "You saw Kate?"

"You don't know?"

There was an accident, she said, another fire. Dylan and Kyla had thrown a party at the Hendersons' mansion. Twenty-two people had died, and nineteen of them were Gibson students.

"Twenty-two?"

She started listing the names of the students, and he was surprised that he knew almost all of them and relieved that he felt as terrible as he did. He barely paid attention to the students. At work, they were a job, and at home, if he thought about them at all, it was usually with resentment.

"We should do something," he said. "All of us teachers—we should get together and do something."

"Yeah, okay," she said, sniffling. "Maybe."

He was filled with a sudden desire to have sex with her, but he felt like it would be in poor taste to suggest it. "You okay?"

"Not really," she said. "Could you come over?"

When he got to Marcie's house, she was wearing sweatpants and a pair of glasses he'd never seen before, and her eyes were red. Over the break, she'd painted the living room walls turquoise and installed white crown molding. They hugged each other, and she cried into his shirt. He was surprised by what she knew about the students. Kyla had been planning to take a summer road trip to California; Dylan had a sister with special needs; Connor Rivkin was the only child of two high-powered dads, neither of whom had ever taught him how to ride a bike.

"You're a good teacher," he said, sincerely. "You care about the students."

She shrugged. "They're kids, you know?" she said. "They can't help the fact that some of their parents are assholes."

He sat beside her, chastely, until he couldn't stand it any longer, and then he put his hand on her knee and began to rub her leg. "I missed you," he said. "I don't know why."

"Very funny."

"You make me crazy," he said. "It's not even that pleasant. I sort of wish it would stop."

She smiled at this, but he could tell he was making her uncomfortable. He guessed that this was probably the last time they'd have sex.

She took off her sweatpants and long-sleeved T-shirt, and then her bra and underwear, and then sat on the couch, naked. He knelt down between her legs and kissed her until she was wet and moaning. Then he picked her up and had sex with her against the wall. He put his hands under her butt and pulled her against him, pushing inside her as far as he could go. In his mind, he was calling her a slut and a whore, but he told himself that this wasn't really what he meant.

The Forever Homes were crisscrossed with police tape and moving vans. The mansion owners had cut their electricity lines, and behind the fading afternoon sun that bounced along the glass, the houses were dark. The Henderson's mansion was white-paneled with large bay windows. It looked brand new. Along the driveway, people had left flowers and bright metallic balloons, and a pink sheet of poster board with the words "You Were Loved."

When Ethan got home, Keppler was in the lobby, as if he'd been waiting for him to come back.

"Can you believe the company's fighting it?" he said. "Did you read that e-mail from Joe? It's unbelievable."

There was a joy to his disgust.

"I haven't processed it all yet."

"Yeah, sorry," he said, but he kept talking.

When Ethan finally got inside his apartment, it was quiet and felt unfamiliar. He stood in the hallway for a long time, his back against the cool white wall. This felt like a dream, and Nebraska felt like a dream, but where was the place that felt real? He thought about the millionaires who were still living in their giant toxic homes and about Marcie, who was probably alone right now, missing Kate, and about his sister in Nebraska, telling him to want less, need less, how this could make you happy. She had made it sound easy, as if desire was a manageable thing. As if it were possible to crave something without inviting a combustible substance into your body, a thing that would lodge itself inside you, waiting to ignite.

Kindness

She's in Phoenix, at a café/gift shop inside the Greyhound Station, where she is supposed to be meeting her daughter who is late or maybe not coming or possibly dead. Who can say? The station is large and echoing with high ceilings lined with exposed beams and giant air ducts that look like concert speakers. A disorganized line has formed in front of one of the gates, and border patrol agents in army green uniforms are checking IDs. Maybe Anna did show up but got scared? She wishes she had her smartphone to look for an e-mail, but it's at the hotel, locked in a safety deposit box along with her credit cards and most of her money. Instead, she's left with the burner phone she bought in case of an emergency—numbers for hospitals, morgue, jails, drug rehabilitation centers (ha!) all plugged in but useless for contacting her daughter, who, if she has access to a phone, has not shared the number. She loops through the building, then comes back to the café and buys a bottle of water.

Anna's father, who has been divorced from her mother for nearly a decade, is in a windowless exam room in Chicago, snipping polyps from an anesthetized retiree's colon and thinking about Samantha Pearson, the twenty-six-year-old woman who is suing him for medical malpractice. Or rather, who is *probably* suing him? "It's still early," his insurance rep has assured him. "Most of these things never make it to court. Review your files. Keep your mouth shut. Don't panic." He's not panicking, not really, but there are depositions being held, expert witnesses being called, and Samantha Pearson, a woman he diagnosed with hemorrhoids a year and a half ago is dying of rectal cancer.

She's slumped against a column with her husband, Dave, swimmy with heroin and watching two Hispanic kids beat the claw machine. A round-faced boy in a Teenage Mutant Ninja Turtles T-shirt and a pigtailed little girl, young enough to stand there unselfconsciously with her round belly sliding out of her shirt. Dave is sleeping, and she is almost sleeping but determined to keep her eyes open and stay in this last clean bright stretch of the day before her mother arrives. The kids have already snagged a bouncy ball and fluorescent pink stuffed animal that looks like a cross between an alien and a teddy bear, and now she wants them to get the iPhone. She focuses her energy, wills the talons of the machine to be strong and benevolent. After two more tries, they run out of coins, but the delight on their faces stays intact. They scamper back to their mother and show her their spoils—a stuffed animal and a rubber ball—the very best that could possibly happen.

Evelyn's about to give up for the day and is honestly feeling pretty good about giving up for the day, treating herself to a Phoenix minivacation—green enchiladas! Shopping!—when she does one more loop through the building and spots Anna by the video games, sitting on a heap of dirty backpacks with Dave. She's frail with sallow skin that stretches tight across her bones. Sunken eyes. Stringy dark hair. She's so emaciated that her face looks misshapen, ghoul-like. Her eyes are half closed and she seems to be hovering between wakefulness and sleep. Did she look this bad a year ago?

It takes a moment for her daughter to notice her and then another moment for her mouth to slide into a sarcastic woozy grin. "Welcome," she says. "You made it."

"You weren't at the café."

"True," she says, her voice thick and sluggish. "We got kicked out. The two of us are bad for business."

Samantha's attorney is ten blocks from the hospital, so he types the address into his phone and walks through the hustle of commuters to a tall glass-windowed building not far from the Picasso. In a narrow courtyard, two young guys in suits stand beside a stone ledge smoking while a woman in a Staples shirt paces back and forth, nodding her head and smiling into her phone. It's early still, and a crisp breeze whips through the buildings. He double-checks the address and makes himself wait five minutes.

If the case goes to trial, it will take months, maybe years. He will lose money and sleep and hours and hours of his life, and then twelve strangers who have not been to medical school, who may not have even finished *high school* will decide if his medical judgments about Samantha Pearson were sound. In three years, he will be old enough to retire, and Samantha will be dead, but his wife, Stacey, will still be in her forties, and his kids, well, *this* set of kids, will still need to go to high school and college, and someone will need to pay for it. If he's not careful, he'll work until he's seventy.

Anna has been addicted to drugs for twenty years and heroin for almost ten. Evelyn's not sure exactly how long she's been homeless, but she would guess four years, maybe five, about however long Dave's been in the picture. She's thirty-six, and in all likelihood, will never get sober. Evelyn knows this—how could you look at the facts and not know this?—but she is determined to keep being her mother. Once a week, she sends an e-mail, and once a year, she flies to Phoenix, rents a cheap hotel on the south side, where her daughter almost blends. She lets Anna shower and sleep, replaces her clothes and worn-out sneakers with used ones that are functional but have no resale value. Then she goes home.

Some visits, Anna says, "Of course you kicked me out. What could you do? If I had a kid like me, I would do the same thing," but most of the time, Anna is mean and exhausting. She wants something, and Evelyn won't give it to her; she needs to address the wounds from her childhood—"You know that time I broke my arm, and no one believed me for two days?"—and Evelyn, who has heard these complaints over and over again, won't listen. Everything is urgent, escalating, unbearable. And then there are the times when she's out of drugs and money, pacing around the room, scratching at her skin. "Why won't you help me? Why don't you love me? Why do you want me to die?"

If she were a braver person, Evelyn knows she would cut Anna out of her life entirely, but she can't bring herself to do it. What if these are the final days? What if this is the very last chance to be kind?

Because her mother refuses to let him into her rental car or her hotel room, she has to leave Dave at the bus station to fend for himself. For four days, she will shower in a hotel room and sleep in clean sheets, and Dave will get exactly nothing. He is her husband—her real and actual husband—but her mother treats him like a pestilence.

"I love you," she says, hugging him against her, kissing him on the mouth, and although this is partially for her mother's benefit, her feeling for Dave is genuine. To be with him is to be at peace; to be away from him is to suffer.

He slips his hand into her back pocket. "I love you too, baby," he says. "Try to stay happy."

She lets go of Dave and falls in step with her mother, and it occurs to her that her mother has no idea what she's feeling— no idea what she's asking of her—because her mother has never truly been in love. She stares at her—a small narrow-shouldered woman with a puff of gray-blonde hair moving daintily through the bus station, a crosshatching of wrinkles between her eyebrows from six decades of Catholic guilt and worry, a belted denim dress that makes her look as if she's going to a picnic, and all of a sudden, she is overcome with pity: her mother has never truly been in love.

The insurance rep has told him several times that it's within his rights to attend every deposition, but now that he's in the conference room, sitting across from Samantha and her legal team, drinking a cup of watery coffee he picked up at the reception desk and struggling to make just the right amount of eye contact with the people on the other side of the mahogany table, it's hard not to feel like a spy. "When you're in the room," the rep said. "People are motivated to tell the truth. If you can be there, go. If you go, wear scrubs." Samantha Pearson is tall and yellow-blonde with close-set blue eyes hidden behind a fashionable pair of thick-framed black glasses and a wide, raw-looking mouth. She's wearing hoop earrings, a fitted black blazer with the sleeves rolled up to the elbows, a black T-shirt splashed with a silver design that brings to mind a laser show. Except for the chemo mouth and the pale gray skin, she looks like any other twenty-something you'd see on the El, listening to headphones and holding a bag from Whole Foods. Beside her, a worried, ruddy-faced woman, who is surely her mother, peers at him and frowns.

Outside, it's midday, blistering. Within moments, she can feel the hair at the crown of her head burning. Dried palm fronds skitter across the parking lot, and heat shimmers along the blacktop. The sun is blinding. Anna wants to know why she can't be nicer to Dave. "Please," she says, her voice more determined than angry. "Can you just try?" She wanted her to buy him a twenty-four-dollar Phoenix map book from the gift shop that he would undoubtedly return later for cash—is she stupid?—and she is also upset that she has refused to drive Dave downtown to the library. When Evelyn points out that he didn't have to accompany her anywhere that was out of his way, Anna balks.

"He's my husband," she says. "We need each other."

Evelyn wants to say something snide—"Ah, the poetry of codependency!"—but she reminds herself that arguing with Anna about Dave is pointless. In her mind, he will never be anything but good. What is it they say in Al-Anon? Don't talk to the problem about the problem?

About once a day, every day, there is an hour or two of perfect brain time when she is calm enough to think but not yet so calm that her mind falls asleep. If she focuses, she can latch on to these hours, and solutions will come to her like fireworks unfurling in slow motion. *Do this. Don't do that.* It's here—right now, while she's edging past parked cars with her mother, fingering the pills inside the Ziploc bag that Dave's left in her back pocket, the heat blanketing her air-conditioned skin—and she's wasting it. There are practical matters to address—money, of course, supply, transportation between her mother's hotel room and Dave—but her favorite thing to think about is her philosophy of human need, which is what she calls the questions she asks herself about the relationship between what people have and what they are willing to give away, what people are willing to do without and what people, at all costs, believe they must keep. So far, she has scraps of a pattern. She has noticed, for instance, that people who believe that they are lucky are the most generous. She has also noticed that businessmen without wedding rings spend a lot of money on shoes.

The last time he was in a room like this one, he was arguing with his wife of almost thirty years about alimony. At the time, it had seemed important to avoid funding her hopeless crusade against their daughter's drug addiction. He'd been upset with Anna, who had recently stolen a laptop from her brother Jared, who was in the middle of a college semester that was already not going well, and he was upset with Evelyn, who was totally and completely incapable of setting boundaries. They would agree not to buy anything for Anna until she got sober or not to answer her phone calls after 9 PM or not to let her come to family gatherings—but inevitably Evelyn would cave. All Anna had to do was claim that whatever she wanted them to give her was essential to her sobriety, and Evelyn was helpless to say no. "I know I'm stupid," she would say. "I really do know that, but what if she's finally ready to get help, and I'm not there?"

The air in the car is dizzying hot, and Anna smells awful. Body odor, plus a damp rotting smell like a gym bag left in the rain. She's wearing a stained long-sleeved T-shirt advertising a Phoenix half-marathon that took place six years ago and a pair of khaki cargo pants with Velcro flaps above each pocket. Her clothes, along with a bright orange hiking pack nestled between her knees, are threaded with holes and coated in pale yellow silt.

"You want to put your bag in the trunk?"

"No."

Anna stares at her blankly for a moment, as if surfacing from a dream, and then says, "You know what I notice? Poor people will share with each other, but rich people are stingy. Why is that?"

She finds this tangent—one of Anna's favorites—to be particularly irritating. She starts the car and rolls down the windows, waits for an SUV to move past her so she can back out.

Anna squints at her. "Next time you see somebody asking for food, look at who stops. It's almost always a young person or a black person or some lady in a beat-up car. If it's a white guy, he's never rich."

She makes this speech proudly but in a listless, plodding voice, as if her tongue is numb, and then she stares up at Evelyn, waiting for a response.

"I'm not sure I follow."

"Yes, you do."

"People like me and your dad are stingy, but you and Dave—"

Anna shakes her head. "It's just that people like you don't *know* you're rich," she says. "That's all. You can't feel lucky because you don't know anyone less lucky."

She gives Evelyn a gratified smile and then curls her body toward the door and closes her eyes.

"I know there is something wrong with me," Samantha says, reading from an e-mail she sent to a friend a year and a half ago. "But after waiting three months for an appointment with this guy, he wouldn't listen. I said, 'My stomach hurts, and I'm bleeding, and here is a chart I made with all of my symptoms, and here are the articles I found about colon cancer that sound a *lot* like what I'm experiencing, and maybe you could please give me a colonoscopy?' and he just stared at me like I was a type of neurotic female he'd seen before. 'That's from the *Dr. Oz Show*,' he said, right away, like I had just revealed something very dumb about myself, and then my turn to talk was over and he was explaining the improbability of what I was saying and the much greater likelihood that my stomach pains were menstrual and that the bleeding was hemorrhoids."

Although they've been divorced for a long time now, she hears her ex-husband's voice in her head. All the time, really, but especially when she's in Phoenix. "As long as you don't think you're helping," he tells her. "As long as you understand that all of this is really about *you*." For him, cutting off all ties to their daughter was not just reasonable but compassionate—the only real chance she had of getting better. "Whatever makes her comfortable delays her recovery," he would say, as if he, too, wished that he could help their daughter but was restraining himself out of duty.

To be fair, he had tried. There had been years of rehab and counseling, a second mortgage to pay for it all, but as soon as he was done trying, he hadn't looked back, hadn't seemed to question himself once. And this was *years* ago, when Anna was still employed, still in an apartment. How had he been so sure?

She follows her mother past a coin-operated laundry room and an empty dimly lit lobby to a "snack station" filled with microwave dinners and pints of Ben and Jerry's. Her mother collects the healthiest of the options—trail mix, granola bars, low-salt pretzels, yogurt—and then rings a bell for an employee. The hotel is the kind where people stay when they are traveling for jobs that don't pay very well. The floors are all cheap linoleum, bordered with gray plastic baseboards that seem to anticipate huge spills, but everything is newish and clean. In a different life, back when she was still young and pretty and working full-time at IKEA, she used to come to a place like this with a Mormon guy named Levi who sold bathroom products to office buildings and liked to fuck her from behind with the blinds open. Six feet of sturdy blonde Mormon, borrowing against his lifetime of clean living in order to "get the devil out of his system" before he turned thirty. He liked the frankness with which she talked about sex, and she liked the ease with which she could shock him. She was about twenty, but with him she felt old. They did a lot of coke together, which he was somehow always able to supply, and talked about the wife he was sorry to be cheating on and his recent doubts in his faith, which were clearly a torment unequaled by anything else he'd experienced so far in his life. Once, high on molly, he had confessed that, although he'd never been with a guy, he was pretty sure he was gay.

Upstairs in the hotel room, she hands Anna a new pair of cheap cotton ankle socks and underwear along with the long-sleeved T-shirt, sports bra, and track pants she purchased the day before at Goodwill and then washed on the first floor of the hotel. The T-shirt is lime green, which at some point was Anna's favorite color, and has a picture on the front of a sun and a moon along with the Greek letters of a sorority. The back of the shirt says "Tenth Annual Dance-a-thon."

"Cute," Anna says, in a voice that might or might not be sincere, and then, right there, in the middle of the hotel room, she strips off her clothes and hands them to Evelyn, who will throw them away in a dumpster on her way to the airport. This is their deal—new for old. She's wild-looking, ravaged. Dark puffs of hair have sprouted under her arms and between her legs. Her bones look tiny and sharp, and her skin is dotted with scratches and bruises and scabs, a nasty cut on the inside of her forearm that looks infected. A rosy slab crusted with yellow and red. It reminds her of fatty half-cooked bacon.

"What?" Anna says, and Evelyn realizes she's staring.

"Your arm." She reaches for Anna, who pulls away as if scalded.

"I know I'm ugly," she says. "I don't need to be reminded."

As a favor to her mother, she doesn't bring heroin to the hotel and relies instead on pills, which are harder to get and more expensive. Also, they take forever and in the meantime, she gets edgy. In the bathroom, she swallows three of the pills from Dave— fentanyl?—half a Percocet and an Ativan to calm her nerves.

They wait for the elevator in a black marble hallway and look out at the sprawl of the city bordered by the blue stripe of Lake Michigan. Samantha and her team are still in the conference room, but the defense attorneys speak to each other as if she is beside them, listening. Weather, Cubs, weekend boating plans. Inside the elevator, they all stare straight ahead in silence while they descend twenty-six floors. In the lobby, an attorney half his age grips his hand and thanks him for his time.

Then he's alone in the sunlight with two hours to kill before he's due back in the office. He thinks about calling his wife, Stacey, but she'll worry or worse placate him—and what he needs instead is practical level-headed advice. He mentally scrolls through his friends from med school, residencies, current colleagues, and then he thinks of his ex-wife's sister, Georgia, who is head of obstetrics at Northwestern, and who he knows for a fact has been sued at least three separate times. It's a bad idea—she's just on his mind because this lawsuit has put Evelyn on his mind—but she really would be perfect. Smart, cold-hearted, incapable of saying anything simply to be nice.

For the rest of the morning and most of the afternoon, Evelyn and Anna sit propped up in separate double beds, watching hotel cable with the blinds closed and the air-conditioner pumping. First, a romantic comedy, then three episodes of *Law & Order*. It feels a little like being in a hospital room and a little bit like being held hostage. She gets Anna to eat a bag of pretzels and drink a glass of the chalky hospital-grade rehydration powder she picked up at a travel clinic in Naperville. "It's so hot out here," she keeps telling her daughter, as if the issue is simply Arizona, as if every resident of this state is in just as much danger as Anna. She would like to take her to a doctor's office to get antibiotics for that cut, but Anna thinks it's a trap and refuses to go.

Back at work, he tries to do paperwork but can't concentrate. He told Samantha to follow up in two months and she didn't. It's in the chart; it's part of the record. The point of dispute is simply whether he presented this follow-up visit as a necessary precaution or as an effort to humor a nervous patient. In other words, he's being sued because Samantha Pearson thinks he's an asshole. He's inclined to stop attending any of the legal proceedings aside from what's required of him by law, but maybe he's missing something.

He opens the internet browser on his computer and finds the website for Georgia's department and Georgia's wide-eyed headshot. She's older than Evelyn, and therefore him, by about five years but has a prim no-nonsense look about her that makes her seem as if she belongs to his parents' generation. Long iron-gray hair striped with white. Heavy features. A strong jaw. Or maybe it is just that he always saw her the way Evelyn did—as an older, all-knowing big sister. He wants her to tell him what to do. He dials her office number and gets a receptionist who offers to take a message.

"I'm a physician," he says, pausing, aware that he is waiting for her voice to change.

Dave is a beautiful man. Dark hair, pale blue eyes, a face that makes you think of a movie star. It's the cheekbones, mostly, but also the sneaky smile, the way he flashes his grin like just the two of you are in on the joke. When they walk together, holding hands, she can see how people look at him first and then her, assessing the gap. But what she loves about him most is simple: he loves her, the real her, the one that most of the time she is trying to hide. He has seen her puke and shit and scavenge through garbage. He has watched her steal skateboards from school children and take drugs from a dead friend's body. He knows that she has sold sex for less money than it would cost a family to eat lunch at McDonalds. He knows that she has been careless enough to get sent to jail on multiple occasions, and he knows that in her adult life, she has never voluntarily been sober for more than eight days. And what he says about this all is that of everyone he's known in his life, she is the most brave.

Her hair is not yet dry from the first shower, but she takes off her clothes a second time and steps under the hot water. She needs to think. Dave's pills have made her feel as if she has been sucked up into a hot air balloon and is floating above the room. She feels unsteady but also clearheaded. They have calmed her mind and brought some things into focus. For instance—maybe she will go to the hospital and get medicine to make her arm stop itching. The shower has a half glass door, no tub, and a plastic tube of liquid soap that's hooked around the metal pipe of the showerhead so that it's impossible to steal. According to the bottle, the soap can be used as both body wash and shampoo. It smells like cheap cologne. She lathers her hair into a tangled squeaky-clean mess and rinses it clean and scrubs the skin on her arm until it bleeds.

Anna has promised not to bring heroin into the hotel, but it doesn't take a genius to know that she's lying. How else to explain the fact that she's been in the bathroom for forty minutes? Why is Eveyln so stupid?

"Mom, I'm used to it," Anna had told her, rolling her eyes. "You think I can take needles into the shelters? I'll manage."

Outside, it's still bright, but the neon signs in the glass storefronts of the strip mall glow orange and pink. "Bikini Coffee." "Smokin' Lingerie." Someone's returning a semi to the Budget rental car lot across the street, trying unsuccessfully to straighten out the trailer. She knocks on the bathroom door.

"Anna?"

Nothing.

"If you don't answer me, I'm unlocking this door."

He's at home, unloading their industrial-sized dishwasher, packed to the gills with several days' worth of plastic plates and sippy cups, and talking about storage containers with Stacey who's sitting at the breakfast bar flipping through *House Beautiful*. She wants to redecorate the playroom but thinks it will cost too much money to do it right.

"Look at these shelves," she says, pointing to a picture of white cube-like shelving inside a closet. "Guess how much they cost?"

"Two hundred?" he says, aiming high. The answer is eight.

"Do you think they're really any better than these things I found at Target?"

Most of their conversations are like this—polite surface-level conversations about whatever is directly in front of them. They rarely argue, and when they do, it almost always ends quickly and without yelling or tears. Some of this is Stacey, an only child raised by two nearly elderly parents who is almost always willing to give in to avoid conflict, but some of it is the new married version of him, a guy with a second chance who knows how easy it is to fuck things up.

She unlocks the bathroom door with a disassembled ballpoint pen and finds Anna sitting on the bathroom floor, her shirt half off with her head between her knees. She looks like she's trying not to throw up. She kneels down beside her, and puts her hand on her back.

"Are you sick?"

Anna makes a low groaning sound but doesn't answer.

"Talk to me. Are you awake?"

She's cold, barely breathing. She puts her arm around Anna and starts to help her dress herself, but something's wrong. The uncovered arm is the one with the cut on it, and the cut is wet, open, oozing.

"What did you do?"

From a distance, as if she's underwater, she hears her mother threatening to call 911, but her mother's body is sitting too close, clawing at her, and her breath smells like onions.

"Mom?" she says. "*What* are you talking about?" Or at least that's what she means to say. She can't tell if she's actually spoken.

"Your arm," her mother says. "Where is the needle? You injected something into that cut!"

She tries to explain that she is just dizzy, that she *didn't* bring heroin or needles to the hotel, that her mother has no idea how hard she has tried to be good, but her voice doesn't work.

"Anna," her mother continues. "Get *up.*"

Her mother is crying, sobbing really, mascara running—who knew that her mother *wore* mascara?—and she is devastatingly disappointed. Anna, once again, has failed.

She calls 911 and reminds herself that, honestly, this is probably a good thing. Anna has done something stupid, but now she will get help. Antibiotics, drugs to counteract the heroin, and then, who knows? Maybe this is the scare that she needs. She sits beside Anna on the bathroom floor and puts her arm around her. She means to say that she's worried, but she hears herself yelling.

"What the hell's wrong with you?" she says. "Do you want to die?"

Over and over again, she says this, though the more she yells, the more she knows the answer is obvious. Yes, probably Anna does want to die, and maybe, deep down, if her daughter really isn't ever going to get better, this is the thing that Evelyn wants too.

She can feel herself being lifted and she can hear a man's voice saying something and her mother is still crying. There are flashing lights, sirens, palm trees. She's here, but she's also dreaming. There's a tall peach-colored hotel, and she's there with Dave and Levi—the three of them together in a big bright room. She's on the bed, wearing a long flannel nightgown like the ones her mother used to wear, legs pulled into her chest, and Dave and Levi are standing in front of her, naked.

"Go ahead," she says. "Dave doesn't mind."

"It's true," he says. "I don't."

Levi kneels in front of him. The whole thing looks like a sacrament, and Anna, looking down at them from the bed, is the angel.

"You're gay now," she tells Levi. "Okay? This, my friend, is your chance for a new life."

In the back of the ambulance, she sits on a plastic fold-down bench by the doors while a paramedic with a handlebar mustache tries to resuscitate her daughter. There's an IV in her hand, a bag of oxygen above her face, but she is still not really breathing—not deeply or often, not enough. His coworker—a young woman with thick black hair and penciled-in eyebrows—asks Evelyn the same questions she has already answered, her voice calm but persistent. Is there a purse somewhere? A pill bottle? A cell phone? Besides the opioids, what did she take?

He's on the couch with Stacey, watching *Property Brothers* when his cell phone rings with an Illinois number he doesn't recognize, and then he remembers, *Georgia*. He hears his voice stammering as he sneaks away to the front office, bracing himself for a lecture. This, after all, is why he called. He wants her to yell at him. He wants her to say, "You are not just a bad doctor but a bad man. You abandoned your wife and your daughter. You think you've gotten away with it, but you haven't."

He sits down in the leather chair and takes out a leather notebook and thanks her for calling. But her voice is uncharacteristically gentle—a whisper, almost. Is she crying?

"Hello?" he says. "I can't hear you."

"I'm here," she says, a tiny, distant, voice, and he realizes that this is not Georgia but Evelyn. Illogically, he pictures her at the yellow house that they used to own together, sitting cross-legged in the middle of their bed, pleading with him to give Anna another chance. A sleepless night, Evelyn red-eyed, distraught with emotion, determined to stay awake and resolve their dispute. She had seemed, in those last years, like an impossible suffocating presence—unable to compromise, unwilling to ever let him go. Back then he had hated her, wanted her to know how much he hated her, and now? Now, he would do something differently, but still, for the life of him, he can't say what.